T0339690

GATEKEEPER

GATEKEEPER

BOOK ONE IN THE DAEMON
COLLECTING SERIES

ALISON LEVY

Published by SparkPress, a BookSparks imprint,
A division of SparkPoint Studio, LLC
Phoenix, Arizona, USA, 85007
www.gosparkpress.com

Published 2020
Printed in the United States of America
ISBN: 978-1-68463-057-8 (pbk)
ISBN: 978-1-68463-058-5 (e-bk)

Library of Congress Control Number: 2020906193

Book design by Stacey Aaronson

For Matt and Eric

CONTENTS

PROLOGUE

The pounding rain soaked through her clothes in seconds, washing away the blood on her shirt and hands. Her shoes were soggy and made her feet heavy as she sprinted through the city streets. Panting, she ran blindly, with no idea where she was headed in the darkness, only conscious of what she was running from. The adrenaline flooding her veins drowned out her grief. She felt nothing but terror.

"Run!" The memory of her father's final command reverberated in her ears. He had shouted it at her as he grabbed the man with the knife. But she hadn't run then. She'd still been crouched over her mother.

THE UMBRELLA SHE held shielded the violent struggle from her view. She held her mother and wailed.

"Mom!" she screamed. "Oh God, Mom!"

At first, she begged—begged her mother, begged God, begged the red gush of blood—while she pressed her hands over the wounds, as if trying to force her mother's life back into her limp body. Then, barely hearing her own voice, she began to apologize. She apologized for arguing with her mother that morning. She apologized for not studying for the exam. She apologized for sneaking out with her friends after curfew. She would never do it again. She was so, so sorry.

When nothing she said triggered a change, she began to sob. "Mom! Mom!" The blood spreading over her mother's green blouse slowed from a gush to a trickle. Her wet, red hands trembled as her eyes inched their way to her mother's face. "Mom?"

Rain beat down on her mother's dull, unblinking eyes.

Her chest constricted. She could only breathe in tiny gasps. The world fell away, reduced to a muffled blur, as she stared at her mother's body. The wild pounding of the rain on her umbrella drowned out the rest of the world, filling her ears with a dull white noise. With every labored breath, she expected to wake up from this nightmare. It wasn't real. It couldn't be real. This sort of thing happened to other people—not to her, not to her mother. It was all a mistake.

It wasn't until her father shouted her name several times that she remembered the assailant. As she lifted her gaze from her mother's corpse, the world came back into focus, and when she glanced out from under the rim of her umbrella, she saw two men locked in a violent struggle barely two steps away. Blood from a dozen red slashes ran all over her father's arms. He had the young attacker by the wrist and was holding the knife at bay, but the man was fighting hard to get free.

Only then did she realize that the killer wasn't looking at her father. Far from concentrating on the struggle at hand, the lean young man was staring with heart-stopping intensity right at her. And his eyes were blazing with murder.

Her broken heart pumped out cold terror. The umbrella

slipped from her trembling fingers and fell to the ground; its dark canopy spun for a moment before it tipped onto its side and came to rest in a puddle. Her father bellowed at her again —"Run!"—and this time she jumped to her feet. Jolted by the stranger's glare and her father's desperate shout, she bolted.

TIME PASSED IN gasps and footsteps. She had no sense of whether she had been running for blocks or miles. As fatigue overtook her muscles, the memory of her mother's dull stare overtook her mind. Soaked to the bone, she came to a stop, hot tears streaming down her face and mingling with the cold rain. Her mom was dead. This new reality of her life wrapped its long fingers around her brain and dug in its claws.

She let out a pained sob and sank to her knees. Through heavily blurred vision, she glanced around, barely registering the tightly packed old buildings and cobblestone street. She stared vacantly at the distorted reflections of the streetlamps' glow in the rain-stained sidewalk. The illuminated water flowed into the cracks between the paver stones and over the edge of the curb, draining into the road. It looked like a painting that had been splashed with paint thinner and left on the wall to run and drip. The storm beat down upon her. Her tears streamed through her long, unbound hair as she wrapped her arms around her torso, giving herself the hug she would never again give her mom, and let out a deep moan.

A car sped past, its headlights barely penetrating the downpour, and splashed a puddle over her. She was so drenched that she hardly felt the water, but the noise of the vehicle brought her out of her mournful trance.

Still shaking from exhaustion and misery, she got to her feet and looked back the way she'd come. The rain and her tear-filled eyes made the world a dark, wet haze.

"Daddy?" she called out.

As far as she could see, she was the only living soul on the street. She squinted against the storm and took a few steps in the direction of the scene she had fled.

"Daddy?" she said again.

The only response she got was the drumming of the rain. For the first time, it occurred to her that she might have lost both parents in the same night. Even when she had seen her father struggling with the killer, she'd never once thought that he might die. Her father—a large, strong man—was invincible in her eyes. She couldn't fathom that he would ever be beaten by anyone, especially a man threatening her life. What outcome could there be but that he would fight off the stranger and then come to rescue her?

But he hadn't come.

Her grief was suddenly overpowered by fear. Without her father, she had no family left. Without him, she was alone.

"Daddy!" she shouted as she started to run. "Daddy, where are you?"

A shape came out of the night, shuffling through the puddles, obscured by the curtain of rain. She hurried toward it, her desperate mind filling in the details of the outline until it looked like her father.

It wasn't until she was a few strides away that the truth asserted itself and she skidded to a stop, arms flailing and eyes wide. The man was too young, too tall, and too lean. It wasn't her father.

The stranger's murderous gaze locked onto hers again, and

he lifted his knife. She opened her mouth to scream, but mortal terror choked her; all that escaped her lips was a squeak. In the light of the streetlamp, the killer smirked.

She pivoted on her heel and scrambled away like a mouse that had just stumbled upon a coiled snake. At the far end of the block, she spotted another man and headed straight for him.

"Help me!" she shrieked. "Help me, please!"

The short, heavyset man turned in her direction, and she felt a flush of hope and relief: she had been seen. She glanced back at her parents' murderer and saw him walking, almost casually, toward her.

"That man!" she yelled, pointing. "He stabbed—"

With her eyes on her pursuer, she never saw the blade that slid between her ribs.

On the ground, gasping like a fish on the floor of a boat, she stared up at the pitch-black sky. Pain radiated outward from the stab wound in her chest and encompassed her entire body like a cocoon. The storm pelted her with its emotionless tears and washed away the evidence of her wound even as it oozed from her veins.

Two men appeared on the edges of her vision, her parents' attacker and her own. Their unfamiliar faces peered down at her with identical, bland expressions.

"Just the girl?" asked her assailant. "Where's the other one?"

"Dead," the younger man replied. "Husband, too."

Daddy? A fresh wave of pain seized her body; lava-hot tears scalded her eyes.

"This kid's the last one, then." The older man leaned over her and squinted down through a pair of glasses. "There should be more of a dent in the dimensional barrier by now."

"I don't know what you're talking about," the young man

said through a yawn. He scratched at his neck with the hilt of his knife. "'Dimensional barrier,' 'last one'—nothing you people say makes much sense."

"Just answer me this: Is there anyone else in the family? Another daughter? A sister? An aunt?"

"Both of the parents are only children and this girl's their only kid. I killed every other relative on the list you gave me. The whole family's a dead end."

The whole family.

Her eyes swayed from one man to the other and then to as much of the world as she could see from where she lay on the street. A blaze of light cut across her vision, accompanied by the sound of tires slicing through puddles. She opened her mouth to call for help, but as she drew breath, blinding pain shot through her torso and quashed her voice. The car drove up the street without slowing. The two men showed no sign of concern at its passing.

"If she's the last," the older man said as he carefully scanned the area around her bleeding body, "then there'd be a breach opening up about now. But there's not." He sucked air through his teeth and shook his head. "Fuck." He took out his phone and, leaning forward to shield it from the rain with his body, typed a message. "There's another one somewhere."

"Another what?"

"Gatekeeper."

"More weird terminology," the younger man griped. "Whatever. You want me to kill someone else?"

"Doubtful," the older man said. "We did a very thorough search of this branch of the family. It's more likely that the gatekeeper we want is abroad. We'll get someone to find her and then send another one like you to finish the job."

"Another one like me?" The younger man chuckled. "How many murderers are on your payroll?"

"Too many," the older man replied with obvious disgust.

The wiry young killer snorted and casually waved his knife in the older man's direction. "If you people don't like it," he said, "then do your own dirty work. Or are you above that sort of thing?"

"Clearly not," the older man said, and she saw him nod down at her. "Just because we dislike violence doesn't mean we aren't prepared to do what's necessary." His phone chimed and he looked at the screen. "Our world needs to change," he said as he typed, "even if that means that yours has to burn."

As he put his phone away, he glanced down and briefly locked eyes with her. She gasped and tried to turn her head to avoid his eyes. He quickly looked away. "She's still alive," he said to the younger man. "Take care of it."

Daddy's not coming for me, the girl thought as the man leaned down with his knife in hand. *No one's coming for me.* The blade that had killed her parents hovered before her eyes. It was shiny and clean. *It should have so much blood on it,* she thought. *How can it be so clean when it's killed so much?*

The knife flashed in and out of her sight. She knew he was stabbing her, but the pain was like a distant echo. Blood loss had left her body numb; she felt hollow and cold. The two men vanished from her dimming sight. She vaguely heard them talking about the weather as their voices retreated.

Her eyelids were heavy, but she stared up at the black sky one last time, wishing there were stars. A primal voice in her mind whispered for her mother one last time before she closed her eyes and finally let go.

1

SKIPTRACE

Rachel opened her eyes, feeling off balance. As her brain cast off sleep's foggy blanket, she glanced around the room. Through the gap in the curtains, a sliver of light drew a buttery line across the armchair, the patchwork area rug, and one corner of the coffee table. Dust floated through the beam like plankton in the ocean's depths; the smell of it was thick in the air.

She glanced at her watch. It was early evening. The beam of light was all wrong. The sunlight usually came through the opposite window at this time of day. That meant the sun had risen over the wrong horizon yet again. *Just one of the "fun" things about living in this house,* she told herself. She drew a deep breath and pushed herself into a sitting position. Her back was stiff, but a quick walk around the house would probably be sufficient to put her muscles in proper working order. If only the path of the sun could be so easily fixed.

Wait . . . what woke me up?

Her cell phone, perched on the back of the sofa, was buzzing softly. She reached for it and pressed her thumb to the screen. The surface stayed jet black as it scanned her thumbprint; then it sprang to life with a bright and colorful glow. Immediately, it informed her that she had three text messages from Wu.

5:02pm
You're late for assignment.

5:28pm
You missed assignment.

5:29pm
You're screwed.

"Crap." She scowled at the phone's clock, still happily ticking away despite having passed the programmed alarm time without so much as a buzz. She stretched her arms over her head, and a shiver raced through her body. With a sinking sensation in her gut, she realized that the temperature had dropped as she slept. Either the heat was broken again or the solar panels couldn't pick up enough light to power anything with the sun on the wrong side of the house.

"Your alarm didn't work," she said to the phone, "I missed assignment, and the heat's out. What are you going to do about it?"

The phone glowed pleasantly, indifferent to its failure. Rachel made an obscene gesture at the screen and turned it off.

She yanked her fingers through the tangles in her dark brown, shoulder-length hair before—still grumbling—she pulled it into a ponytail. She was sorely tempted to chop it all off once and for all. There were strict appearance guidelines for those in her line of work, but some rules had relaxed recently. Short hair on a woman was no longer odd, so cutting hers wouldn't amount to that worst of all offenses: standing out in a crowd. And having one less petty annoyance in her day was tempting.

On her way to the front door, she ducked into the hall bathroom and checked her reflection. Her hair was in decent order, and her face—small, and the color of almond cream—was clean. Satisfied, she strode around the corner to the foyer, donned her old coat, and shoved her small feet into her boots before throwing open the front door and trotting down the front steps of the old house.

On the sidewalk, she paused to glance back at the hole in the cross-hatching beneath the porch. Two little eyes reflected the light—pinpoint ghosts gazing out at her from the safety of their tomb. That stray dog was still living in the crawlspace. She never fed it, never spoke to it, and had never even gotten close enough to it to know what breed it was, yet it seemed attached to living right underneath her nose. It was a wonder the animal didn't starve to death.

Drawing a deep breath, she looked up. The sky was mostly clear—only a couple of clouds drifting through an otherwise lovely blue—but what she saw was meaningless. This place was a scoop of substance dropped into a sea of infinite nothing. The weather within this tiny sphere of existence and the weather in the larger reality bore no relation to each other; they were like two sequential channels on the television: next to each other in order but playing entirely different programs. She was about to change the channel.

She walked a few yards down the front path, toward a point where the walkway faded like a smeared chalk drawing. Just a stone's throw from the house, it was as if everything just stopped. The colors of the grass, the sky, and the clouds all blended into a sunlit smear at the edges of the dimension, as if reality had melted slightly and run together like wax. Just beyond that point, the mingled colors drizzled and faded until there was nothing but an off-white blur that extended into eternity. This was the boundary of the pocket dimension. As she approached it, fog engulfed her. In a fraction of a second, it went from being wispy and gray to thick and dark like the smoke of an oil fire. She took one more step, and it became an ink blot that swallowed everything in view.

No matter how many times she experienced this, Rachel always ended up feeling as disoriented as a sparrow underwater. The path to the house should be behind her, marking the short route she had traveled, but there was no path in her wake. Another step would put a new road under her feet. But here, in this instant, no path existed. Here, her skin was the very boundary of reality. It wasn't just that she was the sole inhabitant of the universe; she *was* the universe. All else was oblivion, the unpolluted vacancy of all.

Her spirit fought the disconnect, just as it did every time she walked this path, by reaching out, searching the empty black for some tuft of substance. But there was nothing. It was empty. Dark. Nothing.

Another step took her out of the threshold space. Rachel emerged into a thin alleyway that ran between two houses. A whiff of freshly cut grass and engine exhaust tickled her face as a flickering streetlight assaulted her eyes. There was a distant shout, followed by a laugh, a slamming door, and the hum of a car passing by a block or two away.

These new sights, sounds, and smells provided an anchor for her disoriented senses to latch on to. Her mind relaxed, her spirit settled, and the stress of that one step subsided, dormant until her next trip through the nothingness.

RACHEL PASSED BY a Greek restaurant, trying not to smell the aromas drifting into the street. Her stomach rumbled anyway, reminding her that she had not eaten since lunch. Against her better judgment, she inhaled deeply. Hummus, lamb, so good . . . She turned the corner and, holding her breath, jogged to the back of the building. There were two doors before her, spread about five feet apart. One door was ajar, allowing the rich scents of spice and meat and the sounds of a busy kitchen to waft out into the back alley. The second door, a dull gray slab covered with splotches, was leaning against the wall, unattached to the building. That the door had been left alone by restaurant employees and passersby alike for so long was unsurprising: it was heavy and grimy, and creepy-crawlies scurried everywhere when it was disturbed.

With a quick glance around to be sure no one was watching, Rachel quietly slipped between the hingeless door and the wall.

When she crossed this threshold—one not unlike the one she'd passed through after leaving her house—she stepped into an entirely different place. The smells of the restaurant vanished immediately, replaced by the stagnant sterility of an office. Clattering dishes and bellowing chefs gave way to the echoes of footsteps on tile and muffled voices from behind closed doors.

Rachel crossed the floor without bothering to look at the dozens of doors that lined the long hallway. Most of these doors had faded words painted on their glass panels, declaring the door to be the entrance to such-and-such street or this-or-that department. None of these were what she had come for. Her boots clunked with each step on the large, speckled white tiles, half of which were cracked or chipped, that led to her destination.

At the far end of the hallway was a tall wooden desk, its surface dotted with stains. Behind it was a set of swinging double doors made of frosted green glass. The faded black letters on the door read SKIPTRACE & COLLECTION. Rachel came to a stop at the desk, glanced around, and, seeing no one, casually leaned her elbows on the rough surface.

"Who's on desk tonight?" she asked loudly.

A gray-haired man bolted up from behind the counter, and Rachel, startled, let fly a string of colorful but unrelated curse words. She drew a breath to calm herself, silently reflecting that she sounded just like her grandfather.

Heedless of her foul language, the gray-haired man squinted at her with wrinkled eyes. "Ms. Wilde," he said hoarsely, "you are very late."

"Yeah, I know," Rachel said. "I fell asleep."

"Asleep?" he exclaimed. "You slept through assignment?"

"Yeah. Sorry, Mr. Creed."

He stared at her, slack-jawed, until she shrugged and added, "I'm an idiot."

That explanation seemed to satisfy him; he snorted and reached out to switch on the screen attached to the wall next to the desk. When it glowed to life, he touched a button that brought up a display of a long list of files, each with that day's date attached to it.

He pointed to the list with one large, callused finger. "There's been quite a pileup lately. Means more work for you lot. Everything on this list has been assigned except for the top four."

"Four?" Rachel asked doubtfully. "That many jobs, I miss assignment, and I only get four?"

"Yes. What does that tell you?"

Her stomach sank as she read the look on Creed's face.
"That all four of them really, really suck."

"Exactly so." He highlighted the top four files and held out
his hand.

With a resolute sigh, she handed him her phone.

He touched it to the screen and then returned it. "Here
you are."

Rachel thumbed through the new files on her phone. The
first two jobs looked unpleasant, mostly because they would
be time consuming, but they were pretty standard.

"I'm gonna need some special equipment for the first one,"
she said, waving her phone at Creed. "These things aren't just
hard to catch, they're almost impossible to hold on to."

"Right, right," he mumbled. "I knew that. Wait a moment."
He walked through the door behind the desk and disappeared
for several long seconds. When he returned, he was carrying a
box that resembled a small pet carrier, except for the barely
perceptible shimmer of green that covered the tiny barred windows. "You've used these before, right?"

"Yeah," she said, taking the carrier by the shoulder strap.
"Thanks."

She opened the third file and immediately wrinkled her
nose. "This mark's human."

"Correct."

"Is that really appropriate for our department?"

"Not my call," Creed said. "Not yours, either."

"I don't like human marks," she said. "Couldn't I trade it
for another job?"

Creed laughed. "If you'd been here for assignment, you
could have argued for a better caseload, but you're late. And
even if you'd been here, you would have had a hard time get-

ting someone else to take that case. Every collector present this week avoided it."

"Shit," she grumbled. "All this because I took a little nap."

She opened the last file and squinted at the contents. "'Gate-keeper?' Aren't all gatekeepers monitored by the Central Office?"

"Normally, yes."

"Well then, let the Central Office track them down."

"It's a 'her,' actually. And it's *your* job to track her down."

"How?" she exclaimed. "Unless there's a name or address—"

"There isn't."

"Fuck!" Rachel kicked the desk. "It'll take me more than a week to finish all this!"

Creed shook his head at her like a parent silently scolding a whiny child. "Show up on time next week."

"Peachy." Rachel snatched up her phone and the carrier and flashed a fake smile. "Thanks. See ya next week."

She turned, carrier in hand, and marched back down the hallway. She did not look back.

PETTY THEFT

If she could finish at least one of the jobs on her docket that night, Rachel reasoned, then maybe, just maybe, she could finish the remaining three by the end of the week, before next assignment. After ducking out of the checkpoint office, she slung the carrier over her shoulder, tucked her phone into her pocket, and power walked up the avenue. She had a daemon to catch.

Her journey brought her to a neighborhood heavily populated by failed businesses with boarded-up windows and padlocked doors sporting FOR SALE signs. Small groups of people loitered in front of the old store windows, some loud and jovial, others eyeing Rachel with suspicion. She ignored them all, even the group of young men who followed her for half a block making obscene comments. Her focus did not waver. She had a job to do.

When she arrived at the address in the file, Rachel immediately saw why this subject had been labeled "defective"; the daemon was living in an empty building. Petty theft daemons were supposed to inhabit areas where shoplifting was a genuine temptation, such as supermarkets and shopping malls. Working properly, the daemon should have been loitering by a display shelf, whispering through the ether into the ears of unseeing humans, tempting them to snatch something and walk off with it. However, in an empty space like this one, there was simply nothing to steal. Clearly, though, the damaged daemon was still trying to perform its function: the unoccupied building had been broken into repeatedly by passersby who were lured by the daemon's siren call.

Those people were probably pretty disappointed and confused when they found there was nothing to steal here, Rachel thought with a chuckle.

Every daemon had a function in the fabric of the universe, whether to draw humans to virtue or to vice, and when they malfunctioned, that natural order was disrupted. A theft daemon trying to lure people to an empty building wasn't serving its purpose, and therefore needed to be repaired. For that to happen, Rachel had to catch it.

She slipped on a pair of gloves made of thin but durable material before climbing through a broken window and pulling the carrier in after her. The carpet beneath her boots was stained and faded beyond color. The empty building smelled heavily of mold and urine. Gnaw marks in the drywall and feces in the corners told her there were animals living in the walls. *Rats*, she guessed as she set down the carrier. *Or maybe squirrels.*

She pulled a pair of tinted glasses out of her pocket. When she put them on, the eyewear shifted her perception until she could see into the ether, the unseen layer of reality that permeated all. The image the glasses provided was slightly out of focus but clear enough for her to process what was before her.

Pulsing colors and waves of visible air moved through the room everywhere she looked. Ghostly shapes shimmered in and out of existence like starlight. Thousands of churning particles swirled around her as she walked the perimeter, bouncing off her skin and clothes, slowly tumbling every which way in strange and intricate patterns. The wall that hid the probable rodent infestation was vibrating with orange tremors, humming with life, as the creatures behind it went about their business without regard to her presence.

Rachel absentmindedly licked her lips. So far, all of this looked perfectly normal. She glanced at her hands; they were glowing slightly in the soupy, ethereal air now that the gloves had had time to draw on the energy within her body to charge the fabric.

Over the tops of her fingers, she spotted the tracks—two parallel rows of tiny, iridescent spots in the far corner of the room. She crossed the floor, followed the tracks to a half-rotted door, and pushed her way into the neighboring room. A flash of relief hit her, followed quickly by a slow build of expectation for the challenge ahead.

There, walking up the wall, was the petty theft daemon.

Its wrinkly skin was a blue overlaid with a gold-glitter shine that sparkled when it moved its foot-long, larvae-like body. It had ten skinny, centipede-like legs along the sides of its tubular body that ended in sharp points rather than feet. Large, triangular eyes covered its bulbous, pug-faced head, making it damn near impossible to sneak up on. Rachel knew from experience that these daemons were squirmy, quick, and very nimble. She sighed. It was going to be hard to catch.

The daemon blinked half of its eyes at Rachel and immediately began to grunt and hiss. It was speaking.

Rachel, born with a rare ability to understand the chatter, felt a stab of annoyance. The daemon had recognized her as a collector and was protesting its innocence.

"You have a defect," she said.

"No broke, no broke," it insisted. "Working, working."

"Get in the crate."

"Working."

"Get in the crate!"

Its ten sticklike legs trembled wildly and then it took off, scrambling across the wall as swiftly and deftly as a cockroach on steroids. Rachel groaned and charged after the creature.

"I don't want to chase you, you grubby-looking freak!" she shouted.

"No broke."

"Yes, you are!"

"Working."

"Shit!" she said. "Fine, we'll do this the hard way. Hold still!"

The daemon raced in erratic circles around that room, and then the next one, and then yet another one after that, but it never tried to leave the building. Rachel spent over an hour chasing it. She pounced on it various times, only to see it tirelessly wriggle through her gloved fingers. She was exhausted, starving, and pissed.

She fumed as she watched the daemon scurry across the ceiling at an intimidating speed after escaping her grasp for the hundredth time. *This is gonna take all night.*

But then, just when she was ready to collapse, the daemon was distracted by an elderly man hobbling by the building. Noticing him, it stopped in its tracks and instinctively began to whisper its temptations to its unsuspecting victim.

While it whispered, Rachel pounced. Her charged gloves gripped the daemon's wriggling body. The creature shrieked and fought to get free, each skinny leg waving and stabbing the air, but Rachel quickly thrust the thing into the carrier before it could escape.

"There!"

"No broke, no broke."

"Oh, shut up!" she hissed at the carrier.

The daemon threw its body against the sides of the carrier, rocking it back and forth, but the thin layer of energy that coated the inside prevented its escape. Rachel watched through scowling eyes until the daemon subsided. True to its nature, it accepted the change of circumstances and became calm after just a few seconds. Just as the abandoned building had once been, the carrier now became its whole world.

Rachel heaved a sigh of relief and wearily slung the carrier's strap onto her shoulder. She took off her glasses and tucked them into her coat. Then she pulled back her left glove and checked her watch.

"It's not too late. I should scope out the next job, get a jump on my work for tomorrow. Hey you," she said to the daemon as she headed for the broken window, "behave yourself."

The daemon didn't move and didn't make a noise.

THE STATION

A bus arrived, its blazing headlights slicing through the darkness and its digital sign displaying the word DOWN-TOWN. Rachel rose from the bus stop bench, her weary muscles groaning, and stood on the curb as the vehicle approached.

The bus driver held up his hand to stop her as she came up the steps. He pointed at the pet carrier. "Service animals only."

Rachel held up the carrier for him to see inside. He peered through the bars and saw nothing but a vacant box.

"It's empty," she lied. "I'm just returning it to a friend."

Satisfied, he waved her inside. She sat down near the front and placed the carrier on the seat next to her. Inside, the daemon hummed contently, singing its song of enticement to the other passengers. Most ignored it, but one young lady, no more than fifteen years old, inched a little closer to Rachel and snuck a peek inside the carrier.

Finding it empty, the girl frowned, looking confused and disappointed, and turned away. As the daemon's whispers continued, she cast her eyes about the bus until they fell upon an older lady near the front. She had fallen asleep, and her arm had slipped off the purse in her lap, leaving the open top unguarded. The girl slid out of her seat and into the seat next to the sleeper, her eyes fixed on the purse.

While the bus lumbered its way through the city, Rachel checked the file on her phone that described her next assignment. It wasn't nearly as specific as the file describing the theft daemon. It contained a list of strange sightings and encounters that had taken place over the last week at The Station downtown: weird shadows, bodiless noises, objects moving on their own, and a handful of less obvious transdimensional episodes. Rachel groaned quietly. She now understood perfectly why no one else had wanted this assignment.

She semi-consciously brushed her stomach, where a three-inch, lumpy scar commemorated her first encounter with a daemon that had been too much in this world. Facing this daemon made her nervous. She had been fortunate the last time because Suarez had been with her; they'd still been rookies then, working in pairs. This time, she was working alone.

"Something tells me you're not gonna help me if I get hurt," she mumbled to the pet carrier.

The daemon within crooned mindlessly.

Rachel closed the file on her cell phone and quickly sent a text to Wu, Suarez, and Benny, the three collectors she had partnered with during training.

Headed to The Station, she texted. *Check in on me soon, okay?*

Within two minutes, each man had sent her an affirmative response. That eased her mind a bit. It wasn't the same as working with a partner, but it was better than being alone. Her fingers left her scar and rested on her leg.

IT WAS STARTING to get dark when Rachel walked up to The Station. Huge archways marked where the old railroad tracks had once brought travelers into the structure, though the tracks were now gone and their foundations had been paved into roads, driveways, and parking lots. Elegant gas lamps had long ago been converted to electric and decades of soot had been washed from the building's stone exterior to bring the historical edifice into modern use as a business center and event venue. Rachel wrinkled her nose and clucked her tongue. *What a waste.*

There was a wedding reception taking place inside. It was a lavish affair. The concourse area was packed to the brim with jovial wedding guests, all smiling happily, glasses in their hands. The already ornate walls were hung with flowers and banners, all of them very precisely arranged to add to the ambiance without detracting from the historical beauty of the room. Large, round tables covered in white cloth and expensive dishes were perfectly spaced to allow maximum seating while still providing a view of the antique marble floor. Above the impeccable room was a vaulted ceiling with a long, translucent skylight that, despite the cloudy sky, filled the room with indigo evening light. The guests mingled and laughed, making the room boom pleasantly with their talk.

Rachel stood in the hallway just outside the concourse and scanned the room through the cracked-open door. Nothing looked out of place. She fished around in her pocket for her glasses, but before she could put them on, a slick black limousine pulled up outside. An excited ripple went through the crowd, and the guests pushed past Rachel with cameras in hand to get a picture of the newlyweds as they came into the building.

All the extra movement was enough to persuade Rachel to wait a few minutes before putting on the glasses. Instead, she moved out of the way and watched as the glowing young bride and her new husband entered the room to claps and cheers. The bride immediately ran to embrace an older man, probably her father, while her husband shook hands with dozens of people. Everyone looked delightfully happy, but Rachel wrinkled her nose. She couldn't help but wonder how much time and money had gone into this night.

Thoughts of her family's last celebration—the day Rettie, her nephew's mother, joined their clan—drifted into Rachel's mind. Rachel's aunt had done all the cooking, filling the house with the rich scents of spiced goat meat and roasted potatoes. Her father had herded everyone who was lured to the stove by the appetizing smells out of the kitchen and kept them busy setting up borrowed tables, no two of which were the same size or shape, in the backyard. Guests had trickled in for hours, all wearing whatever clothes they had worn that morning, until the entire town was in attendance. Rettie had stood for the formal initiation on the back porch and then immediately walked ten feet to one of the tables and sat down to eat. A few of the neighbors had shown up with instruments and provided an impromptu concert that made everyone dance until the yard was nothing but mud. At the end of the party, everyone had taken home a portion of the leftover food.

The memory made Rachel sigh. Just five more months until she could go home.

The hubbub settled down a bit as the couple and their well-wishers headed into the dining hall. Emboldened by the quiet, Rachel put on her glasses, poked her face through the door, and looked around the room.

An explosion of colors and visible vibrations assailed her eyes and made her head throb as she scanned her surroundings, but nothing looked out of place. There were daemons at the wedding, but that was normal; daemons gathered in any place where humans gathered. At a glance, she saw a petty theft daemon climbing a wall; two swirly joy-maker daemons springing from tabletop to tabletop, inspiring guests to dance and sing in delight; and a googly-eyed lust daemon whispering in the ear of a groomsman who was chatting up a pretty wedding guest. A few other daemons moved about the room, but all were behaving normally.

Rachel removed the glasses, adjusted the shoulder strap of the carrier, and walked down the hall, away from the wedding venue. She made her way to the far end of the hallway, past a string of black-and-white photos tracing the history of the building, and took a seat near the entrance of a small, smoky bar.

Now what? She sighed, closed her eyes, and rubbed her aching forehead. She would have to search the area more carefully. If only she knew for sure what she was looking for. As things stood now, she was working blind.

Her phone buzzed. She checked and saw a text from Benny. *You there?*

She smiled a little, feeling a touch of home reach out to her in this strange land.

Still here, B, she wrote back. *No mark yet.*

She pocketed the cell phone and tapped her fingers on the carrier. Where to look? Well, she could start with the bar and then the restrooms. After that, she would have to start trespassing in employee-only areas—something she hoped to avoid, since it increased the risk of exposure.

Grumbling but resolute, she pulled the carrier's shoulder strap into place and was about to stand up when she felt a tug on her pant leg. She looked down and was stunned to see a pile of dirty clothes at her feet. It appeared to be gripping the edge of her coat.

She tried to pull away, but the heap clung to her and refused to be dislodged.

"Uh . . . yeah?" she quietly asked, not sure what else to do.

"Catch?" asked a small, raspy daemon voice.

During Rachel's training, one of her instructors had told her that "Catch" was a term daemons used in reference to humans sent to collect them, but until now she had never been addressed as such. Typically, daemons did not address people at all unless confronted. They simply weren't wired that way; they were nothing but cogs in the cosmic machinery.

Rachel glanced around. When she was confident that no one was paying attention, she leaned over. The pile of dirty clothes shrank away from her face but stayed rooted to the spot.

"Yeah," she said. "What are you?"

The pile did not answer her. Rachel reached down and lifted the corner of a shirt from the top of the heap. At first, she saw nothing but a hollow area in the center of the pile, around which the clothes seemed to be suspended in midair. She put on her glasses and the picture immediately changed. Within the pile, she saw a large, protruding eye looking up at her. It was surrounded by a few visible patches of green skin. One large pointed ear—also green, with a pinkish tint on the inner rim—stuck out of the rags at an angle. The small hand gripping her pants was green and meaty, its three gnarled fingers tipped with pink-and-black claws.

Rachel's skin prickled at the clarity of the sight. Viewed

through her glasses, most daemons looked just slightly out of focus, like objects in a watercolor painting, but this one was as clear as a photograph. It was wrong.

"You're a riot daemon," she said.

The daemon cocked its head at her like a dog hearing a distant whistle. "Catch hear?"

Her skin prickled again. Just as daemons always looked a little out of focus, their voices always sounded a little distant. This daemon's voice was too close to her, almost like a human voice. However, when it spoke, the words seemed to echo slightly, as if it were standing on the edge of a canyon. While its unnatural proximity to her made its voice clear, its words spilled downward into the gaping hole that its emergence into this world had created.

"Yeah," she said, "I understand you." She yanked her sleeve from the daemon's claws. "Do you realize that you're physically affecting the human dimension?"

"Yes."

"Are you doing it on purpose?"

"Yes."

"Do you know you're not supposed to do that?"

"Yes."

"Okaaaay." The desultory conversation was beginning to irritate her. "So, why are you doing it?"

"Think not well."

"You don't 'think' you're well?"

"Yes."

The word twisted in her ear like a screwdriver. *Think?* Daemons were incapable of thinking. They tempted humans; that was all they could do, and they did it with the single-minded stalwartness of bees gathering nectar. But this daemon looked up at her through layers of dirt and discarded clothes, and she saw conflict in its bulging eye.

"Stop work," it said.

"Why did you stop?"

"Not want."

"Want?" Rachel repeated in amazement. "You didn't 'want' to tempt?"

"Yes."

"You"—her eyes widened—"'want'? How do you even know that word? You're not supposed to want. You're *supposed* to tempt people. You're a daemon, that's what you do."

"No want," it unhappily insisted. "Want go. Go no fleshes."

"You 'want' to go someplace where there are no humans?"

"Yes. Want."

Rachel could not have been more surprised if a toaster had asked for a cigarette. Staring blankly at the daemon's big, confounded eye, she scratched her own arm, trying to prove to herself that she was not imagining this bizarre conversation. The daemon didn't want to tempt people; in fact, it wanted to avoid humans altogether. Every word out of its mouth defied basic aspects of daemonic existence. Rachel pinched her eyes shut and shook her head. Her stomach was empty, and this strange conversation was making her head hurt. This was a fascinating case, and most likely somebody smarter than her was going to make a detailed study of it.

"Daemon," she said, "I'm going to take you in for correction."

It cocked its head at her and twiched its long ear.

Guessing that it didn't understand, she elaborated. "Correction will make you like you were before you started wanting things."

The daemon stood in silence for half a minute, its long, pointed ear twitching like a horse's tail, its meaty fingers plucking at a button. At last, its colorless eye looked up at Rachel, and it made a bobbing motion from within the clothes.

"Want go. No want want."

She squinted at the daemon. This job was too easy. She began to reach down, and it shrank away from her.

"Covers?"

"Covers? You mean these clothes? Why are you wearing clothes?"

"Want."

"Well, you can't walk around in public like that," Rachel said. "Someone's gonna see you. Leave the clothes."

The clothing mound shuddered, and the three-fingered hand pulled the material tightly around its body.

"No," it said, a hint of surprise in its peculiar voice. "Want."

"I don't care what you 'want.' You have to leave them."

"No."

"Fuck it all!" she said. "Fine. But pick one piece of clothing, just one. I'll have to carry you. I can't walk down the street with a shirt following me. I hope you're smaller than you look."

Once the daemon had dropped its cumbersome heap and wrapped itself in an old, coffee-colored woman's coat, Rachel hefted it up under one arm. It was, in fact, fairly small—barely one foot tall—but it was as solid as a brick and weighed about as much as a chubby toddler. If the confused creature would have stayed in the limited realm where daemons belonged, she could have carried it without feeling the weight, but it either couldn't go back or didn't "want" to, so she got the benefit of experiencing its full mass.

Before she even made it outside, Rachel's body ached from

the strain. She wanted to drop the little green monster, but instead she trudged dutifully out of The Station, the carrier hanging from one shoulder and the abnormally heavy coat tucked under her other arm. Every few steps, her stomach growled like an ill-tempered watch dog, and her arm muscles muttered dark threats of soreness to come.

All this for missing one meeting, she thought irritably.

BACK AT THE Skiptrace office, Rachel deposited the carrier and the coat on the counter and then rattled off a quick summary of her evening to Creed as she brought out her phone and sent a text to her three colleagues. She was looking forward to telling them the story of this collection job, though she wondered if they would believe it—a daemon wearing a coat that wanted to be corrected. It was a little hard to swallow even for Rachel, who had experienced it firsthand.

Creed, on the other hand, readily believed the story and, from the look on his face, found it fascinating. "A daemon that asks to be repaired," he marveled. "That may be a first for this office."

Somewhere behind one of the hallway doors, Rachel heard muffled shouts, followed by a loud crash. Creed, seemingly oblivious to the unseen ruckus, took possession of the petty theft daemon in its carrier. The coat sat on the desk, rumpled and silent, as Creed set the carrier on the floor by his feet and then credited Rachel's account with the two completed assignments. Rachel felt a wave of relief. Two jobs down, two to go. She just might finish up before the next assignment meeting after all.

As she turned and headed back down the hallway, she heard a voice rise above the din.

"Catch!"

She stopped and glanced over her shoulder. From the countertop of the Skiptrace desk, one arm of the coat waved at her, the excess length of the sleeve hanging limply from the end of the daemon's claws.

"Good, Catch!"

Rachel stared at the old coat, momentarily stunned. Then she smiled, laughed in bewilderment under her breath, and waved back at the daemon.

"You're welcome, Daemon."

ALL THE WAY back to the pocketed house, despite the dull headache that gripped her and the dread she felt for the work that awaited her, Rachel continued to chuckle quietly to herself. A daemon had thanked her for her help. It was going to make a great story to tell her family in her next message home. She pictured their reactions as she related the events of the evening. Her mother would shake her head and smirk when she heard about the pile of clothes the daemon had gathered around itself. Her brothers would laugh themselves silly at the creature's strange talk. Her father would be fascinated at the idea of a daemon being self-aware enough to ask for correction. And her grandfather would raise his thin, gray eyebrows and cluck his tongue upon learning that it had actually thanked her for bringing it in. The story would give them conversation fodder for a while.

At that thought, the smile on her face faded. They would

talk about the story for weeks, but she wouldn't be there to hear it.

Rachel stepped into the shadow passage leading to the house and felt the darkness encompass her.

BURDEN

Rachel was eating her second helping of eggs on toast when she heard a soft but persistent knock at the door. Her heart skipped a beat; she never got unannounced visitors.

She hurried through the house, full of anxiety about the possibilities. When she reached the foyer, she took a deep breath and then threw open the door. There was a brief flash of color and movement at the shadow passage as someone exited the pocket dimension. Too late, Rachel opened her mouth to call out to them, but darkness swallowed the visitor before the first puff of breath left her lips.

She heard a slight rustling sound and dropped her gaze to the source. Her brow furrowed at the sight of a rumpled old coat on her doorstep.

"Daemon?" she asked in disbelief.

The woman's coat quivered and lifted itself up. Under the porch, the stray dog's glowing eyes peered up through the cracks in the wood at the uninvited creature standing just a few feet from its den. It growled.

"Catch," said the riot daemon from inside the coat.

Rachel darted back into the house for her glasses. She put them on as she returned to the doorway, and saw one bulbous eye staring up at her from within the folds of the old coat. She huffed and wrinkled her nose. "What are you doing here? I submitted you for correction."

The creature stood in silence, plucking at a button on the coat with its pink-and-black claws.

Rachel was reaching for her phone to contact the Skiptrace office when an angry rumble sounded overhead. Thoughts of the leaky roof pecked at her mind, overriding her discomfort with the creature's presence.

"Get inside, Daemon," she said, stepping aside to clear a path. "It's about to rain."

The daemon obediently shuffled across the threshold and into the foyer. Rachel closed the door behind it as she checked the Skiptrace Department's master board on her phone.

There was a message under her name, one she hadn't seen when last she checked. The message was headed with the emblem of the Central Office.

"To: Wilde Rachel len Wilde," she read aloud, "daemon collector, natural-born citizen of the Arcana, granddaughter of Wilde Brom who is Head of the Clan Wilde in the town of Kritt in the Plains Region of the Northern Arcanum. Subject: riot daemon. Ms. Wilde, the riot daemon you recently brought in for correction is too badly damaged to repair. We have made some inquiries to see if another office is better equipped to make repairs of this magnitude. However, as we suspected, the only people who are possibly qualified for this work are currently in the Arcana. As you well know, we cannot ship this daemon to the Arcana for correction as long as the interdimensional passages are sealed during the yearlong systems check. At the moment, we have too much work on hand to spare any more time and effort on this one case. Since this daemon's defect is relatively benign, there is no need to keep it locked up in your local Skiptrace office, where it takes up much-needed space. However, it would be irresponsible of this department to turn a defective daemon loose. Since you possess the rare ability to understand what it says, we are placing the daemon in your house until the gates to the Arcana reopen or until this office finds time to reexamine the case, whichever might come first. In the meantime, keep an eye on the daemon to be sure its defect does not worsen. So long as it refuses to tempt anyone and does not otherwise influence the human world, it can be safely ignored. Your continued service is appreciated. Many thanks, Central Office of Daemonic Monitoring."

She scanned the message a second time, her nostrils flared. They were placing a busted daemon in her care? She had never heard of such a thing!

"Whose dumbass idea was this?"

The moment she asked the question, she knew the answer was irrelevant. Good idea or bad, she really didn't have a choice. If she refused to let the daemon live in the house, the Arcanan authorities could toss her out of this crumbling heap —or, worse, inform her family on the other side of the gates of her disobedience. Her elder brother was not on good terms with the neighbors (hadn't been ever since he told the Kritt Council Speaker to shove her opinions up her ass); her little sister was institutionalized due to her need for specialized care; and her other brother had his hands full furthering his education and raising a child. Her parents had seemed to be doing fine when last she heard from them, but her grandfather had a bad leg and couldn't do any heavy lifting. Her causing trouble for the Central Office wouldn't make anyone's life easier. Given the circumstances, she couldn't afford to be selfish. The daemon would have to stay.

"So," she said, "what do I do with you now?"

"Do with?"

"Do you . . . need a room or something?"

"Room or?"

"Yeah, a room. Do you need a place to sleep or do you need something to eat?"

"To eat?"

Thoughts of her unfinished breakfast overrode her patience. "Daemon," she snapped. "I need you to be a little smarter, okay? When I ask you a question, I need you to answer. Don't repeat what I said, just answer." She caught her next sharply worded sentence just as it reached her tongue and shut her mouth. *"Temper gets the better of you, Rachel,"* she heard her father say. As he had taught her to do, she shook her head slowly while she reined in her ire.

"See," she began again, her voice level this time, "here's the thing: I don't have a lot of experience with daemons that doesn't involve me catching them and delivering them for correction. I don't really know what daemons do when they're not tempting people. Help me out, okay?"

"Out okay?"

Rachel set her jaw and glared at the rumpled coat. Her blood was starting to simmer again. "What did I just say about repeating what I say?" she said through her clenched teeth. "If you keep doing it, we're going to have a problem. You don't 'want' that," she said cuttingly, leaning closer to the coat. "Do you?"

The daemon shrank away from her and burrowed deeper into its coat. "No want," it agreed.

Rachel's anger began to subside. This, at least, was progress.

"Let's try again. What do daemons do when they aren't tempting people?"

"No do," was the quick response. "No sleep, no eat."

"Okay, that's a start. So what do you need?"

The colorless eye blinked several times as the daemon considered the question. "Place," it finally replied. "Empty."

Rachel's blood cooled and her eyes softened when she heard the dejection in the daemon's voice. Clearly, the creature was as uncomfortable with this situation as she was. She rubbed her forehead and tucked her hair behind her ears as she drew a few deep breaths.

"All right," she said softly. "Let's find you a place."

She led the daemon up the stairs to the second floor, the carpeted steps creaking under her bare feet with each step she took. In her wake, the little green creature hopped from one step to the next, careful to keep its coat tightly wrapped around its bulky body as it went.

At the top of the stairs, Rachel pointed to the left. "My room's there, at the end of the hall. I don't want you in my bedroom or my bathroom, but there are three other bedrooms and a second bathroom up here that no one uses. There's one bedroom right here and two more down that way. You can use one if you want."

The daemon hesitantly shuffled through the open door of the room in front of them and glanced around the tiny space. It was furnished with nothing but a twin bed, a dresser, and one end table. There were two small windows, a closet, and a cracked mirror on the wall that was half-covered by long strips of peeling yellow wallpaper. Past the closet door, which was hanging by one hinge, Rachel could see several pieces of men's clothing on wire hangers—remnants of the last person to be assigned to this house. The room must have been more appealing when he lived here. Now, the continuous leaks in the roof left pools of water in the mattress and chair cushions, and the mold created what Rachel imagined must be thick, if invisible, toxic clouds in the air.

The daemon stood still for a moment and then suddenly shuddered. It backed through the doorway and burrowed down into its coat.

"No," it anxiously told Rachel. "No. No."

She raised an eyebrow. "What's the problem?"

"Fleshes here," it told her.

"No," she countered, a little puzzled. "No humans live here. Not anymore."

"Fleshes here," it repeated. "No want."

There was that word again. *A daemon that wants and doesn't want . . . and it's living in my house.* She huffed and rubbed the back of her neck. "Okay. There are two other bedrooms this way. They're no bigger than this one but—"

"No," it said. "No want."

"So what *do* you want?" she snarled. "Where the fuck am I supposed to put you?"

The daemon recoiled, its coat wrinkling as it endeavored to make itself as small as possible to escape her wrath. Rachel felt another unwelcome stab of pity and worked to cool her temper yet again.

"There's another option," she said. "Follow me."

She led the daemon down the hallway and opened another door, revealing a narrow set of stairs that led up to a third floor. She trotted up the steps, trying to ignore the complaints of the water-stained wood under her feet, and the daemon followed.

At the top was a small attic. The space was cluttered with old furniture, rolled-up carpets, taped-up cardboard boxes, and dust so thick that Rachel's feet left clear prints on the wood floor. She ducked her head a bit to avoid an overhead beam as she waved the daemon into the room.

"How about this space?" she asked it. "It's all I've got. If you don't want to stay here, I'll have to put you in the crawl space with the dog."

The riot daemon shuffled about the poorly lit area. A moment later, it straightened up to its full height. "Yes," it said. "Stay."

"Glad to hear it," Rachel said. "At least up here you'll be out of the way. I don't need you getting underfoot while I go in and out."

"Go in?"

"Yeah, I have to work. I still have two assignments to finish this week. I can't finish either one sitting around here."

She walked down the attic stairs, and the daemon, after a brief hesitation, followed her, bouncing from step to step like a tiny, awkward kangaroo.

"I have to find a guy who's been tampering with interdimensional passages, and I have to find a gatekeeper who has somehow managed to slip under the Central Office's radar," Rachel explained. "I don't have a name or a lead on either one, so I've really got my work cut out for me."

"Catch go?"

"That's right."

"We go?"

She stopped midstride and looked over her shoulder at the daemon, who, a few stairs above her, was almost at her eye level. "Huh?" she said, forehead furrowed.

"We go?" it repeated.

"Uh . . . no," she said pointedly. "Why would you go with me?"

The daemon pointed at her phone.

"The message?" Rachel asked. "What about it?"

"Catch watch," it said, pointing at itself.

She was supposed to monitor the daemon—that's what the message said. Apparently the daemon had been paying attention before. But "monitoring" it hardly meant keeping it on a leash. "You're not going, Daemon," she said. "You're staying in the house."

It tilted its head. A black-streaked pink eyelid slid over its colorless eye, blinking from right to left. Rachel wrinkled her nose.

"Look," she said sternly, leaning over the green creature. "Let's clear this up right now. You will not follow me everywhere I go. I can monitor you just fine so long as you stay in this house. I sleep here and my stuff's here, so even if I go out, you can be sure that I'm coming back. I'll monitor you when I'm here. Do not follow me."

"Catch watch," it repeated. "Catch—"

"Stop!"

The daemon shriveled down to half its size and closed its eye again, but this time Rachel felt no pity for the creature.

"You're only here because I've been ordered to take you in," she said, poking one finger at the daemon's closed eye. "Got it? You are not a houseguest. You are a burden. Remember that. Okay?"

"Yes."

"Good." She ushered it back up the stairs to the attic. "I'm going out soon. You stay here."

"Yes." It shuffled away into the shadows, carving a trail in the thick dust on the floor.

As the daemon came to a stop in the darkest corner of the

room, Rachel's temper subsided. The situation could be worse. At least the creature would be stowed away in the attic and not in her closet. She turned her back on her unwanted visitor and headed down the stairs. It did not follow.

THE STORM OUTSIDE finally broke as Rachel wolfed down the last of her breakfast, and a mad rush of rain plunged from the sky. Along with the frantic pounding on the roof, she could hear trickles of water dripping down in several rooms where the house had failed to keep the elements out. While cleaning up, she wondered if it was raining outside of the pocket dimension. Rain in the pocket dimension did not always signify rain anywhere else, and since she still had two assignments to complete, she had to dress appropriately for the Notan world.

Thinking of those two jobs snapped her mind to attention. She picked up her phone with one hand while using the other to select a local news station on the wall screen—she figured a weather report would eventually appear—located the assignment files on her phone, and sat back down to review the facts.

The human mark didn't have a name, but there was a photo. That alone told Rachel he was Notan and not Arcanan; if he had been from Rachel's dimension, his face would have been identified by recognition software. He was a thirtysomething man who was showing some hints of middle age around his eyes and at the edges of his white-lipped frown. His short, dark hair was graying prematurely, and his bushy eyebrows were a nearly solid gray above his hard eyes. According to the information in the file, he had been trying to open interdimensional gateways. Authorities weren't sure if he was trying to summon something or attempting to travel to some of the dimensional spectrum's other layers. Either way, they wanted him stopped. That could only mean that he had come very close to succeeding. This wasn't some hobbyist messing around with interdimensional passageways for a laugh; he was the real deal.

Rachel clucked her tongue. Collectors weren't often sent after humans, and when they were, it was usually in pairs. That the Central Office had deemed this assignment suitable for only one collector suggested that the man wasn't dangerous. Still, Rachel hated human marks. Daemons, even broken daemons, were fairly predictable, but humans . . . you could never be sure what they would do. And all she had on this man was his photograph. No name, no address, no nothing. There were a few suggested areas to check out in the folder (probably places where he had tried and failed to open a gateway), but they were at opposite ends of the city and had already been checked out. Not very promising.

She opened the other file. The gatekeeper bloodline in question was charged with guarding an ancient Egyptian daemon called Apep. Due to its irreparable defect, Apep had been sent to the wastes, a dimension at the far end of the spectrum where broken daemons slowly decayed and returned to the primordial ooze.

According to the file, many thousands of years ago, Arcanan authorities had severed Apep from its ability to move between dimensions and attached that ability to a human woman. Her descendants continued to carry the ability, unused but never discarded, and that had kept Apep trapped in the wasteland where it could do no harm. One branch of the family had, until recently, lived in Istanbul. Two months ago, the last three members of the family (father, mother, and teenage daughter) had been murdered. The Notan police report called it a probable mugging gone bad. The thief had stabbed the mother first and then fought with the father while the daughter ran. He'd overpowered the father, killed him, and then chased down the girl, whose final screams had brought bystanders to the scene, though not in time to save her life. To the best of the Central Office's knowledge, this unlucky family had been the last descendants of the original gatekeeper chosen to seal the daemon away. But if that was true, then the daemon would have been loosed upon the earth the moment the poor girl's heart stopped beating. Apep was still imprisoned in the wastes, however, and that meant there was at least one living member of this gatekeeper bloodline. Rachel was now charged with finding that living relative.

"How is this even a job for daemon collection?" Rachel grumbled. "Somebody screwed up."

Screwup or not, the job now had her name on it, and that made it her problem. At least for this assignment, she had a possible place to start. With one eye on the wall screen, still watching for a weather report, she closed the file on her cell phone and scrolled down the contact list. When she found the name she wanted, she pressed the send button and held the phone to her ear as it rang.

"Historical records," said a woman's voice, polite but bored.

"Extension 184, please," said Rachel.

"Hold," droned the voice.

While waiting for the connection to go through, Rachel listened to the combination of heavy rainfall outside and dog food commercial on the screen. The dog in the ad was a big, goofy-looking yellow thing with a glazed expression, not at all like the sharp-eyed dogs back on her family's farm. She wondered briefly if the dog under her porch was staying dry in this weather before a series of clicks on the phone announced that the requested extension had been reached.

"Historical records," said a different voice, this one male. "This is Wentrivel Paavo len Wentrivel."

"Hey, Paavo," she said, trying to force a smile into her voice. "It's Wilde Rachel."

"So it is!" he brightly replied. "Well, this is unexpected! How have you been, Rachel?"

The overly friendly tone of his voice did not escape her notice, and she shifted her weight uncomfortably because of it. He was using informal honorifics and pronouns, implying that they had a closer relationship than they did. Rather than get into an exchange of pleasantries, she launched directly into her request.

"I have an assignment with no leads that I don't know how to jump into," she told him. "Does your office keep records on gatekeeper families?"

"Yes," he said, and to Rachel's relief, his tone shifted from personal to professional, his language formality rising a level. "We don't monitor them, though. We just keep records of lineage."

"Can you check on this gatekeeper bloodline for me and let me know if there's a surviving branch on record?"

"Sure." There was a shuffling noise on his end, as if he was moving things around. She heard a computer boot up and then heard the soft *bap-bap* of his fingers on the keyboard. "What's the daemon?"

"Apep. A-P-E-P."

"Got it," he said as he typed. There was a brief pause and then he said, "Apep, also called Apophis." He let out a low whistle. "It's an old one. I should've known it would be. Only the oldest daemons have names."

"The last known gatekeepers died recently," Rachel pressed on, "but the daemon hasn't crossed over. That means the bloodline's not extinct, right?"

"Typically, yes. Let me check something." The keys clacked and he hummed a bar of music. "Hmm . . . I've got the family tree on my screen and it doesn't look good. It's been over four thousand years since a woman was chosen as gatekeeper for Apep, and her descendants have been struggling to hold up her mantle ever since."

"What do you mean?"

"Branch after branch of this woman's family tree has turned up dead over the centuries," he said. "The three murder victims in Istanbul were the only known descendants. Well, the only *direct* descendants," he clarified. "According to our records, the Apep gatekeepership passes only from mother to daughter—duplicating with each birth so each woman holds a copy—so any branches that were the product of male descendants wouldn't be included in this record. Hold on." The keys bapped and blipped enthusiastically through the cell phone as Paavo hummed.

Rachel waited, biting her lip to suppress her irritation.

"Okay," he finally said. "I've found eighteen direct-descent female lines on this family tree."

Eighteen. The musical sound of that number flushed the grating noise of Paavo's hum from Rachel's ears.

"Great!" she said. "Any of them local?"

"Hold on," he said. "Seventeen of them are extinct."

"Seventeen! Are you sure?"

"Very sure. We have confirmed deaths for most of them, and no daughters born to the others."

Seventeen dead branches. Rachel's stomach felt like it was full of lead.

"What about the eighteenth?"

"At first glance, it looks extinct, but we don't have a confirmed death on one female descendant of that particular line. This is probably the bloodline the Central Office thinks is still around."

Probably. The success of this case hinged on a "probably." Rachel cursed under her breath. *Well,* she thought, clenching her teeth, *if "probably" is all I have, then that's what I have to pursue.*

She slumped into the sofa. "So, who's the gatekeeper? Where do I find her?"

"Don't know," Paavo said simply. "All I've got is a record of a woman with a missing granddaughter four hundred years ago."

"Four hundred." Rachel groaned. "Are you serious? If there is a surviving gatekeeper, she could be anywhere in the world. What makes the Central Office think this is even close to the right spot?"

"They've got oracles and those 'otherworldly' types at their disposal," Paavo said. "Someone with higher knowledge must have zeroed in on that area."

Rachel rubbed her eyes and exhaled through her teeth. "Why couldn't that higher knowledge give me a name to work with? I've got no hope of tracking this woman down."

"Well . . ."

Rachel heard Paavo's fingers punching at keys again.

"I think I can narrow down your search a little bit," he said, sounding smug.

"How?"

"The woman you're looking for is of African ancestry."

"Why do you say that?"

"The original missing girl disappeared from a West African town in the seventeenth century. That area was a well-documented site of slave-trader transactions. She was probably sold and transported to the American colonies on a slave ship. I wonder if . . ."

Rachel perked up. "If?"

"If I can find any records of slave auctions around that time," he said. "Records from seventeenth-century America are spotty at best, but there might be something."

The hopelessness of this case weighed heavily on Rachel's shoulders. The more she heard about it, the more likely it seemed that she would be saddled with searching for this gatekeeper for the rest of her term of service. But Paavo was offering to help, and however fruitless his assistance might turn out to be, she did feel a little better knowing someone else was on the job with her.

"That would be great," she said sincerely.

"It's a long shot," he warned her. "Even if I find the girl listed at an auction, you might not be able to find records of her children and grandchildren. Finding a currently living descendant from a slave auction record is difficult."

"It's the best lead I've got," she said. "Would you mind helping me out?"

"Not at all!" he eagerly replied. "I'm just glad to have something to do!"

Rachel noted with dismay that his voice was shifting back to the lighter, more casual air he'd started the conversation with. "My department was the first to be cleared by the systems check, so I've spent the last six months just sitting at this desk. It's wake up, go to work, sit at the desk, go home, and repeat. I'd really like to have more to do, especially in the evenings." He cleared his throat. "How about you? Are you busy most evenings?"

Rachel rolled her eyes. This time he was dropping hints so blatant that it made her skin twitch. From the moment she'd first met him, he had been trying to draw her eye. Still, this was the most forward he had been with her in all the months they'd known each other.

"Yeah, the collectors have a lot to do these days," she said as casually as she could. "Seems like I never have enough time for all my work. Well"—she spoke a little faster, trying to wrap things up—"I appreciate your help. Thanks."

"You're welcome. Hey," he added brightly, "Kash came through here last week with his unit. I asked him about you."

Rachel pinched her eyes shut and silently swore. So that was it. All Paavo's previous flirtations had been dampened by the fact that she'd had a boyfriend; now, that obstacle was gone, and he was ramping up his efforts. *Kash Dhruv, did you really have to run your mouth about our breakup to this guy?* The thought of him soured her already bad mood. It had only been a month since her final confrontation with him; she wasn't ready to be reminded of it.

"I don't want to talk about it," she said, her voice a tad sharper than she intended. "Can we please drop the subject?"

She sensed Paavo pulling back in response to her tone. A few tense seconds passed before he braved the silence with a small, "Sure." He sighed, his disappointment tangible. "I'll look into this gatekeeper thing for you."

"Thanks again for your help," she said, her voice as plain as she could make it.

"No problem. I'll get back to you soon."

Rachel ended the call and, with a sharp exhale, dropped her

phone onto the seat beside her. Dhruv. She'd kept him out of her thoughts for weeks, and now, thanks to a few minutes on the phone with Paavo, he was all she could think about. Fuming, she clicked off the wall screen, forgoing the weather report. She grabbed her phone, her coat, and an umbrella before heading for the door. The people at the Central Office weren't the only ones with access to an oracle. She knew where to find one. It was safe to say that he wasn't formally trained like the Central Office's people, but if she asked him the right question, he might say something useful. He also might collapse in a babbling heap, but she was short on ideas and desperate to redirect her brain away from Dhruv, so she was willing to take the chance.

"Daemon!" she shouted. "I'm leaving! You stay put!"

She stepped onto the porch, zipped up her coat, and closed the door behind her. The rain was thrashing the overgrown lawn into muddy soup. The galloping deluge was so thick she couldn't see the end of the walkway. Taking a deep breath, she opened her umbrella and ran.

The downpour soaked every inch of her clothes not immediately under the umbrella in mere seconds. She ran at top speed to the edge of the pocket dimension and bolted into the shadow that divided it from the larger world. A quick step through the darkness, and she burst into the familiar alleyway.

She stopped in her tracks and lowered the umbrella. No rain. Just bright, sunny skies.

"Shit," she cursed. She looked down at her sopping wet boots and pants legs and realized that despite the sun shining overhead, the chill in the October air made it unlikely that they would dry quickly. She shook off the umbrella, folded it, and tucked it under her arm. Just like that, she would be cold for the rest of the day. *Peachy.*

ORACLE

Someone was coming.

The feeling was faint, a flickering spark in a thick fog, but it was there. He was so adrift in the overflowing sea of his own mind, he rarely felt anything with such certainty. The feeling drew him, pulling him up from the depths of his delusions and giving him the slightest glimpse of sanity. His madness clung to him and weighed him down, keeping him mired in its cacophonic ooze, but beyond the edge of the fog, he sensed the waking world like a silhouette behind a curtain. Patches of reality began to intrude upon his crazed senses—the stink of the river, the jab of the rocks beneath him—as he slowly became aware of his neglected body. A dozen aches and pains stung him, but because he was still half-wrapped in his numb lunacy, the sensation was distant. He hovered there, barely connected to himself, and waited.

She was coming. Coming to see him.

RACHEL SLID DOWN the long embankment and shuffled her way to the belly of the bridge. The tail end of the morning commuter rush was passing over her head, and the wind that whipped up from the surface of the water was colder than an October wind should be, nearly freezing the wet ends of her clothes. She wrapped her arms around her torso and hugged herself for warmth as she trudged on.

A handful of people, ageless and sexless within their bundles of clothing, sat huddled in the small spaces, quiet and still in the shadows cast by the lights above. They glanced silently at Rachel from within their many layers of clothes with bland curiosity, but made no move either toward or away from her.

Glancing sidelong at them, Rachel was eerily reminded of the daemon in her attic and the way it looked at her from the depths of its coat. Like the daemon, these unfortunates seemed to go through life with only one foot in reality—just enough to make physical contact but not enough for others to notice them.

A wool blanket with many holes covered a vaguely human form that was set well apart from all the others. Rachel cleared her throat loudly as she approached, causing the blanket to stir. From one end of the blanket, there emerged a shaggy mop of hair so caked in filth that it shed clods of dirt every time the head beneath it moved. Beneath the hair was an equally dirty face, overgrown with a monthslong beard. The lips within the beard were deeply chapped, so much so that multiple scabs covered the broken skin. The man's age was difficult to determine in his unkempt state, but Rachel estimated him to be younger than most of the others under the bridge.

An aggressive stink—part river pollution, part body fluid—surrounded him like a toxic cloud. Many bruises, some old and some new, dotted his face and neck, signs of the harsh life he lived. But even amidst so many marks of hardship and sorrow, his electric blue eyes were full of energy, so much so that they seemed to vibrate with intensity. When he spotted Rachel, the haze of delirium that was his daily existence seemed to lift and a spark of recognition lit up his eyes.

"Girl doesn't belong here," he rasped. "Wrong world."

Rachel first stumbled across him while chasing a defective daemon along the edge of the river. At the time he was face down and lapping the river water like a thirsty dog. Rachel didn't notice him as she ran after her mark until she accidentally tripped over his legs. They locked eyes as she rose, and immediately the man started on a rambling tirade. Rachel was no stranger to abnormal behavior—her sister suffered from a rare condition that often caused her to act in unfathomable ways—and would have ignored him and gone about her business except that the homeless man's rant included a great deal of personal information about her life. Within seconds, he was shouting the names of Rachel's immediate family, along with a slew of Arcanan words. The daemon slipped away, leaving Rachel on the riverbank with her mouth hanging open as the crazed man raved about her homeland, relatives, and favorite swear words.

After that day, she'd begun to notice him all over the city. For some reason, the delirious oracle had latched on to her; he kept putting himself in her path. On those rare occasions when she sought him out, he was always in the first place she looked. Typical of oracles who did not have control of their abilities, he appeared to live in total mental chaos and did not hesitate to share his insanity with passersby. But for all his outbursts, he had never been violent and had never caused Rachel any serious trouble. She hoped he could help her now.

Seeing the deplorable conditions in which this man lived, Rachel wished she could do something to help. Unfortunately, she was sorely unqualified to help an undisciplined oracle, and those who *were* qualified weren't authorized to interfere in the life of a noncitizen. To speak to him at all was really a border-line violation (not a serious offense, but certainly worth a scolding), but she was willing to take the risk. She had a job to do.

She smiled at the man. "Hello, Mr. Oracle. I brought you something to eat."

She handed him a plastic bag containing an overstuffed beef fajita that was still fairly warm despite her long walk to the bridge. He eagerly took it from her with both grimy hands, tore off the wrapper, and shoved one end into his mouth. Two of the scabbed wounds on his lips tore open and leaked blood into his food, staining the white tortilla, as dribbles of oil and sauce escaped his mouth and further stained his already filthy beard. Rachel flinched at the thought that the salt and spice in the fajita were getting into his wounds and probably hurting the poor man pretty badly. But the oracle showed no hint of pain; he devoured the fajita in less than a minute and, once finished, reached for the drink in Rachel's other hand. He gulped down the soda—pausing only to belch—and then carefully set aside the cup like it was a precious thing made of paper-thin glass.

"Finished?" she asked.

"Good," he said. "Good food."

"Okay. Can we talk?"

Staring at her with an intensity that made her skin crawl, he pointed between her eyes with one dirty finger. At the end of the finger, a hangnail was held to his skin by a large scab.

"Girl doesn't belong here."

"I know." She backed away from his outstretched hand. "Listen, it's my job to find these two people, but I have no idea where to look."

"Green monster," he mumbled as he picked loose pieces of

meat and bell pepper out of the fajita wrapper. "Wears a lady's coat."

"Yep," she confirmed. She was impressed with his insight but also annoyed that he was focused on the wrong case. "I got that daemon without a problem. It's two humans I'm looking for."

He licked the fajita sauce from his fingers, not seeming to mind that he was ingesting quite a bit of grime along with it. "Keeper," he said thoughtfully. "Looking for a keeper."

"Yeah, a gatekeeper," she agreed, eyebrows raised. "Do you know where she is?"

"Looking for her," he continued to muse, his mad blue eyes —shocking blue, unnatural blue—darting around without purpose. "Lost the other ones. All dead. Last branch of the tree."

"Right." The smell of him was starting to make her nauseous. Fighting the urge to gag, she leaned a little closer to him and pressed, "So where is the gatekeeper?"

"Dog under girl's house," he said. "Puppy. Cute."

"Uh, yeah. So, what about—"

"Good food. Good, good food. From the market?"

"How about the man?" she urged. "Tell me about the man."

"From the market?"

"The food's from a Tex-Mex place a couple of blocks from here," she irritably replied. "So—"

"Market."

"I—"

"Market."

"What market?" she said. "What are you talking about?"

"Little market," he said. "Family owns it, foreign. Little boy, lizards. Supposed to be a restaurant but it's a market. Red and blue over the door."

"Red and blue over . . . oh!" An image suddenly popped into her mind. The corner market a few blocks from the portal to her house, the one where she bought most of her food, had a scarlet awning over its door with a beautifully intricate sky-blue design on it. The market was run by a husband and wife, both of whom spoke with noticeable accents. They had a little boy, six or seven years old, probably American-born, who sometimes played with plastic dinosaurs behind the counter. Was that the market the oracle was talking about?

"What about the market?" she asked.

"Market," he mumbled. He lay down and pulled his holey blanket up over his shoulders. "Food. Keeper. Girl doesn't belong here."

His words devolved into random syllables as he curled into a fetal position. The erratic spark in his eyes dimmed, fleeing from the brightness of reality into the depths of senselessness. His lips moved silently, forming the shadows of words, and his head bobbed gently, as if mimicking the motion of the wind.

Rachel sighed and shook her head. "And that's the end of that. Thanks for the help, Mr. Oracle. Sorry to bother you."

He murmured quietly to himself and rolled over, turning his back to her.

Rachel shook her head in amazement. That this man could rest so easily in his situation was astounding. She almost envied him.

"See ya," she said before turning around to head back the way she had come. "I guess I'm going to the market. Wish you'd told me what to look for there."

The oracle gave no response other than a soft snore.

MARKET

Rachel opened the market door and stepped inside. The heat pumping through the vents welcomed her and wrapped her in its airy joy. For the first time all morning, the numbness in her legs brought on by her rain-drenched pants began to thaw. Her muscles warmed and her skin dried. She exhaled through a smile.

One of the owners, the husband, sat at the cash register flipping through a magazine as Rachel walked in. He was a handsome man in his late thirties with black hair and weather-worn skin. He was thin but had a lively look to him, an inner glow that shone through his russet-brown eyes. A series of small scars covered his hands; Rachel guessed that they were the mark of a kitchen accident, possibly an oil burn. It made her wonder if the oracle's comment about a restaurant had been correct.

A glimmer of recognition flashed through the man's eyes when he saw her enter. "Hello, crazy girl," he said pleasantly with his thick accent.

"Hi, Mr. El Sayed."

Crazy girl. He had been calling her that for three months now, ever since he saw her wrestling a daemon into submission on the curb near his store. Of course, he couldn't see the daemon, he just saw a young woman cursing wildly as she grappled with the air. To his credit, he didn't seem to hold it against her. As long as she paid for the things she got from his store and as long as she kept whatever delusions she might have to herself, he always politely welcomed her into his place of business. Rachel genuinely liked him.

His son was behind the counter too, sitting cross-legged on a child-size chair. The boy's thick black hair was getting a little long; it dangled into his big brown eyes as he hunched over a notebook of lined paper in his lap. His full lips curved into a natural smile even as he struggled to write a perfect letter *K*. Engrossed, he absentmindedly sucked his teeth. He was clearly working hard, because he hadn't even noticed Rachel yet. Usually, he was all smiles and happy greetings when she came in.

Rachel glanced around the store for a clue as to why the oracle had sent her. All she saw was the store as it always was: no wanted man, no gatekeeper. She muttered darkly under her breath and cursed herself for putting her trust in a madman. Feeling the owner's eyes on her, she tried to think of something to say, some excuse for her presence.

"I want to make some burgers for dinner," she said, suddenly realizing that it was true. "Can you hook me up?"

"I am out of beef," Mr. El Sayed said.

"I'm good for beef, but I need tomatoes, cheese, and buns."

"Buns are with the bread, cheese is in the refrigerated section, but I have no more tomatoes. Those kids," he said, his grip on the magazine tightening, "they snuck in yesterday while I was in the back room, and they smashed the tomatoes all over the floor."

"Same kids who spray-painted the front door last week?"

"Yes." His jaw clenched and his eyes flamed. "Three of them this time. When I catch them, they will wish they had never set foot in here."

Rachel had heard more than a little grumbling about these three kids around the neighborhood. In recent weeks, vandalism and theft had been the fate of nearly every business within a six-block radius of the Bell household, the center of operations for the incurable delinquent Bell brothers. Michael, fifteen, and Ian, thirteen, had stepped up their level of mischief since they started including their youngest brother, Freddie, twelve, in their outings. From the gripes she'd overheard, it sounded like the police knew these boys by name and had no shortage of complaints about them, but, unfortunately, they also had a lack of evidence.

Rachel had known a like-minded boy in her hometown. When he was caught vandalizing a neighbor's house, his mother marched him into the next town meeting and volunteered him to every family in Kritt who needed their house painted. It took him months to finish, and by the time he was done, he had lost all interest in paint. Last she heard, he was happily working on his family's farm, pulling his weight without complaint. That was as it should be.

"I've noticed that the businesses around here that keep guard dogs haven't been vandalized," Rachel said. "Those three brats might be scared of dogs."

"I noticed this as well," Mr. El Sayed said, nodding.

"Have you thought about getting one? I've got a stray under my porch that could use a home."

"I cannot," he said with a wave of his hand. "My wife is allergic."

"Oh." Until that moment, Rachel had not noticed Mrs. El

Sayed's absence, but as she glanced around the store, it became apparent that she wasn't there—unusual. "Where is Mrs. El Sayed today?"

"She is upstairs. She is not feeling well."

"I'm sorry. I hope it's nothing serious."

"I think it is the weather," Mr. El Sayed said. "The sudden cold upsets her."

Rachel nodded. The chilly temperature didn't agree with her either, especially while her clothes were still damp. "It's hard to shake off a chill once it settles in, huh?"

"Yes, very." He glanced at her over the top of his magazine. "If you have a chill, there is fresh coffee in the back, very hot."

"No, thank you." The offer of something to drink brought out a craving. "But do you have any cherry cola?"

"Yes, with the other sodas in the back. Third cooler door from the left."

"Thanks." She began to move toward the back of the store, but as she did, thoughts of the oracle haunted her brain, filled her with curiosity, and stopped her in her tracks. She swiveled back toward the counter. "Mr. El Sayed?"

"Yes, crazy girl?"

"Somebody told me that this space was going to be a restaurant at one time. Is that true?"

He blinked, his eyes met hers, and he cocked his head. "Yes," he said in a tone alight with surprise. "Yes, that is true. When Safiya and I came to this country, we intended to open a restaurant, but it was costing us too much money to get started. Who told you this?"

"A lunatic who lives under a bridge."

"Ah," he said with an accepting nod. "A friend of yours?"

"Sort of."

"Crazy people know the strangest things," he said quietly. He turned the page of his magazine and leaned back against the wall. "Enjoy your cola, crazy girl."

She walked to the back of the store, toward the back wall, which was lined with glass-doored refrigerators. She glanced around as she walked down a line of shelves. Canned items were perfectly stacked, cracker boxes stood tall one after the other, and cleaning products sat in the far corner so as not to risk contaminating the food. It was just as it always was. Why the hell had the oracle sent her to this market? What was she supposed to find? It didn't make any sense.

Well, she said to herself, *he was right about the restaurant. He must know something I don't.* With no other leads and no better ideas, she resolved to wait.

The cherry cola was right where Mr. El Sayed said it would be. She fished out a bottle and twisted off the top. It fizzed sharply, bubbles rising to the top. She took a sip, and the bubbles fizzed all the way down her throat.

Drinking cola was like drinking laughter. Soda was impossible to get in the Arcana and customs threw a fit every time she tried to bring a case of it through the interdimensional passages. It was one of the few nice things about being stuck in the Nota dimension. This world made the best junk food.

While her back was turned, the front door of the market opened and a man walked inside. Neither Mr. El Sayed nor his young son took notice of him as he began to pace up and down the aisles. Rachel took another gulp of cola without turning around, but when she lowered the bottle to replace the cap, she suddenly caught a glimpse of the newcomer's reflection in the glass door of the refrigerator. Her heart jumped and she quietly gasped.

It was him. It was the man in the photograph, the one she was supposed to arrest.

Slowly, she turned around. Heart pounding, she quietly moved to the far side of the store, putting as many aisles between her and the man as possible, and tried to decide what she should do next.

Very discreetly, she sized him up. He wasn't particularly tall or muscular, but she was a small woman and he was definitely bigger than her; bringing him in might be challenging. She could tackle daemons all day long, but people were another matter. She, like everyone from the Arcana, had received basic combat training, and her mother had taken particular care to teach her daughter enough fighting techniques to protect herself, but, even so, she was not a soldier. She trusted that the Central Office would only assign one collector to this case if they'd ruled that he wasn't dangerous. But she looked at her target again and felt her nerves twitch. Dangerous or not, she was not looking forward to the confrontation.

Keeping both eyes on the man, she tried to hammer out a plan of attack as quickly as possible. She would prefer to try to convince him to come along quietly, but then he would be alerted to his pending arrest and might run for it. Her best bet was probably to grab him from behind, but that plan didn't sit well with her either. She pulled out her phone and rapidly typed a group message to Suarez, Benny and Wu asking for help.

Just before she could hit the send button, the man walked up to the counter with a jug of orange juice in his hand.

"Thank you, sir," said Mr. El Sayed as he handed the man his change. He glanced at Rachel, and his eyes zeroed in on the open bottle of cola in her hand. "Hey, crazy girl, you need to pay for that."

The man looked over his shoulder and finally noticed Rachel, who was still staring at him. The two of them locked gazes. His jaw tightened (momentarily thrusting out two pale scars on his chin), his nostrils flared, and his eyes narrowed. Rachel's blood chilled and her breath turned to ice in her lungs. Within his eyes, she saw something disturbing. And for the first time since being handed this assignment, she felt fear.

Like a dirty mirror that just barely reflected a faraway candle's flame, the glimmer in the depths of the man's eyes was so dull that it gave no light and no warmth. She had never seen this before but knew instinctively what it was: her target's soul was almost burned out. Not the kind of soul that exited the body at death (a thing Rachel did not believe in and an entirely different word in her native language), but rather that mishmash of conscience, self-awareness, and humanity that defined one's personality and connection to the rest of the species. Where the light of this man's soul should have been, she saw only an open, gaping maw, a never-ending hunger that was devouring him from the inside out. Soon, he would be an empty shell of a man—all hunger, no substance or morality.

The only way a person could lose his soul was through obsession, and nothing fueled an obsession more readily than a daemon. This man's daemon was probably so much a part of his life that it didn't even need to whisper its temptations anymore; the man had given himself over to it so wholeheartedly that he could no longer separate its voice from the voice within his mind. He and the daemon had become one doomed entity.

As Rachel stood there, rooted to the ground, the man grabbed his juice, turned his back, and rushed out the door. His speed startled her. It was as if he knew she was after him. But how could he know that?

Regardless, it was her job to arrest him, and he was getting away.

She pocketed her phone and scrambled to the window. The man was walking up the street at an intimidating pace. She swore under her breath. Unfortunately, the fact that his soul was hanging by a thread meant that he was too dangerous to risk losing sight of. She couldn't wait for her colleagues to respond to a text; she had to catch him now.

"Do your job," she mumbled. "You have a job to do, so do it already."

She dropped the bottle of cola onto the front counter. It wobbled frantically on its end but then righted itself. She was about to bolt for the door when Mr. El Sayed lunged across the register and grabbed her by the wrist.

"Crazy girl!" he said sternly. "That drink is not free!"

"I'll come back and pay for it, I promise," she said, her eyes darting back and forth between him and the front door.

"Pay me now, not later!"

"Mr. El Sayed, I have to catch up with him. It's really important. Please," she added when she saw doubt in his eyes. "Do you really think I'm a thief? I swear on my grandfather's name that I will come back."

Mr. El Sayed stared at her. Then, with a resolute sigh, he released her wrist. She immediately bolted for the door.

"You come back today!" she heard him shout after her. "Today! You pay me, or I will find you!"

Rachel sprinted up the street in the direction she had seen the man go. Her heart pounded in her ears, louder than her thundering footsteps on the pavement and her manic breaths combined. When she reached the corner, she scanned the streets in every direction, but her target was missing.

There were plenty of side streets and dozens of driveways where the man might have gone. With one hand, Rachel fished out her tinted glasses and jammed them on her face, and the world became a wild and colorful place, all the movement, tracks, and activity in the ether suddenly apparent to her. She saw several daemons along the street, all of which were going about their business without noticing her, and she saw the tracks of daemons that had passed by recently. She also saw a faint and smoky line of orangish-red floating before her at chest level, like mouse prints in a surrealist painting, heading straight up the street.

During her years of training, Rachel had been taught to identify many types of daemon trails, including this one, though this trail was technically not from the daemon but rather from the spot on the man to which the daemon had attached itself. Experts disagreed as to what, exactly, the trail consisted of, but they all agreed on one thing: it could only be left by a person who was losing his soul. The man's obsession was providing Rachel with a clear path to follow.

As she ran, the blots of sickly color struck her in the chest and dissipated. The trail turned sharply to the right up ahead, leading down a driveway toward an apartment building. She turned to follow it and suddenly spotted the man just a few yards ahead.

His back was to her. There, attached to the back of his neck, was a squirrel-sized daemon with four needle-thin arms, each about three feet long. Its tiny jaws were buried deep in the man's neck, seemingly into his spine, and its long, long arms were holding the man's shoulders in a spindly bear hug.

Rachel didn't stop to consider what type of daemon it was; she didn't want to miss this chance to catch him off guard.

Without a second thought, she ran straight at the man, arm drawn back and ready to strike.

He whirled around just in time to duck her swinging fist. Her knuckles raked the edge of his coat, knocking something solid from his pocket that crashed to the ground in a noisy bundle of clinks. In one fluid movement, he spun around and elbowed her in the back of the head. The blow knocked her to her hands and knees; her vision jiggled as her brain bumped back and forth inside her skull. Her ears rang like a fractured telephone, but she still heard a jangle of metal as the man scooped up whatever she had knocked from his pocket. As he walked past her, she heard a gravelly voice mumble, "Stupid bitch."

It took a long moment for her to gather all her senses into a functional whole. Finally—head throbbing, body aching—she pushed herself up, slowly, to a sitting position. Holding the back of her head with one hand, she retrieved her tinted glasses from the pavement with the other, put them on, and glanced around.

He was gone. And the fight had scattered the unique ether trail all around the area like blood spatter at a murder scene, making it impossible to tell which direction he had gone. Rachel groaned, but it was just as well. Even if she caught up to him, she now knew that she wasn't going to be able to handle him alone. That move he'd used to put her down—it was the move of someone who had been professionally trained. If she wanted to catch him *and* to avoid another head-bashing, she was definitely going to need help.

She held up her hands, looked at her scraped palms, and winced at the thought of the future pain. She was going to have to scrub hard to get the gravel out of her wounds. She swallowed a mouthful of blood, a gift from her bitten tongue. The taste was repulsively bitter. *"You earned that taste,"* she heard her mother's voice say, *"by acting rashly."*

She looked around and was relieved to see that at least no one had witnessed her getting her ass kicked.

"Stupid bitch," she echoed in self-reproach. "This is why I hate human marks."

She dusted off the front of her clothes and ran her scraped fingers through her tangled hair. She made a quick assessment of her injuries (headache, bloody hands, bitten tongue, bruised knees) and concluded that she was fine. A few scrapes and bruises had never been the death of anyone, and Rachel had sustained worse injuries in the line of duty. A few bandages would fix her up, and she would get right back to work.

There was an ache in her knuckles, strong enough to be distinct from the rest of the pain in her hands, that she didn't know how to explain. *Backtrack and work it out.* Mentally, she relived the moment of her attack in slow motion. Lunge, dodge, elbow to head. *No, back it up.* There was something else, a moment of contact. When she charged at the man, her fist had struck his jacket as she lunged. Now she remembered that her knuckles had hit something hard in his coat pocket, sending it flying. Whatever it was, the target had stopped to retrieve it before disappearing.

"Doesn't make any difference," she said. "He's gone now."

"That."

Rachel's overtasked heart tried to escape through her throat. She jumped up much too fast and backpedaled several steps, her arms windmilling, and her wide eyes fell upon a familiar sight: the oracle from under the bridge. There he stood, mere feet away from her, his shoulders slumped, his filth-encrusted hair obscuring his features, and his abnormal blue eyes fixed on the ground.

Rachel's shock immediately gave way to annoyance. This was not the first time she had run into him unexpectedly, but this was certainly the first time he had appeared after she had gotten her ass handed to her.

"Mr. Oracle," she snapped, "are you following me again?"

"That."

"Following me around is gonna get you hurt!"

"That."

"Do you understand me?"

"That."

She marched up to the scruffy man and grabbed him by the shoulder. The touch seemed to release a wave of foul smells; they wafted off of his body with the force of a boxer's punch, but Rachel didn't recoil. The gut-wrenching stink of him only fueled her anger.

"You can't follow me around!" she said. "Part of my job is blending in! I can't do that if you're following me!"

Even with her shaking him, his attention never wavered from a spot on the ground.

"That," he repeated, pointing. "That."

Close to eruption, Rachel turned to look where he was pointing. To her surprise, there was actually something there. She leaned over.

It was a flash drive. Small, gray, relatively flat, it was almost invisible lying there on the sidewalk. However, it was also in a spot where she would have been almost sure to step on it as she attacked that man. Had she run right over it without noticing? Or had it not been there before?

"Where did that come from?" she asked the oracle. "Did you see?"

"That," he repeated vacantly. He opened his mouth to say it again, but no words came out, and his blank stare was replaced with a look of confusion. He glanced all around, as if seeing his surroundings for the first time. He looked at Rachel and then at her hand on his shoulder. He pointed at her hand. "That."

"What?" She looked at her hand. The knuckles that had struck the target's coat pocket were beginning to swell. "Oh! Was that thing in his pocket, too? Did he leave it behind?"

"That."

"Yeah, I see it."

"That."

"Please stop saying that," she snapped.

He lunged forward and grabbed the flash drive off the concrete. Wide-eyed, he held it up to his face. A foamy saliva droplet fell from his mouth as he stared at it. "Yeah," he rasped. Then, suddenly, he jolted. The flash drive fell from his hand and clattered to the ground as his arms began to flail.

Alarmed, Rachel jumped clear as the oracle collapsed to the ground, his body convulsing wildly. His electric blue eyes stared up at the sky through pinpoint pupils. Rachel shouted a few of the nastier curse words she knew as she hurried to kick anything that was within reach of his twitching limbs out of the way to stop him from hurting himself.

She waited a moment, thinking the fit might pass, but when the convulsions didn't stop, she dashed into the street. "Help!" she shouted, waving her arms at passing cars. "Someone help, please!"

Five cars zoomed past her, some of them honking angrily, but no one stopped. Rachel reached for her cell phone but quickly realized that there was no one she could call. She was forbidden to call Notan emergency services—part of keeping a low profile for her job—and because this man was not an Arcanan citizen, she couldn't call for her people's emergency medical team.

Fortunately for her, the sixth vehicle to turn up the street was a police car. The two officers inside saw her waving erratically and quickly jumped out.

"Something wrong, Miss?"

"That man!" she shouted, pointing back the way she'd come. "He's having a seizure!"

"Seizure?"

"There! He's over there!"

The younger of the two officers ran in the direction she was pointing and found the oracle where he lay trembling and shaking on the ground. He immediately radioed for an ambulance while his partner pulled Rachel aside.

"Do you know this guy?" the officer asked.

"Sort of," she said, agitated. "He's a homeless man who comes around this area sometimes. I don't know his name."

"What happened?"

"He had a seizure!" she said. "He's still having it! Look at him!"

The middle-aged man held up one hand for silence, his piercing eyes silently ordering her to control herself. Obediently, Rachel clamped her mouth shut.

"Did he hit his head or anything like that?" he asked in a voice that Rachel found infuriatingly calm.

"No! He just collapsed!" She took a deep breath, relaxed

her shaking hands, and exhaled through her teeth. "Look, my sister has seizures, so I know what one looks like. There was no triggering event, he just fell."

"What was he doing just before that happened?"

"Standing there, talking to himself."

"Were you with him?"

"I was just passing by," she lied. "He was standing there, mumbling something, and then he collapsed."

"You didn't call for help?" asked the officer, his eyes darting to the phone still in her hand.

"No, I just ran into the street." Hoping that her face showed an appropriate amount of embarrassment, she added, "I . . . I guess I panicked."

The officer nodded—apparently, he accepted her explanation—and instructed her to have a seat on the nearby curb until he could take her official statement before rejoining his partner, who was now standing watch over the oracle.

An ambulance arrived on the scene seconds later, whereupon the officers worked to keep the sidewalk clear of onlookers and to keep traffic flowing on the partially obstructed road. It took just a minute for the EMTs to stabilize the oracle for transport, less than a minute for them to load him into the ambulance, and just one more minute for the ambulance to wail its way out of sight. It took several minutes after that for the two police officers to notice that the young woman who had flagged them down had quietly slipped away, now with a flash drive in her pocket.

7

SHUTDOWN

M r. El Sayed was visibly unnerved by the sight of Rachel's injuries. She handed him her credit card (the bill was paid by the Central Office, provided she didn't make excessive charges), but he didn't immediately take it. Instead, he reached past the card, took hold of her wrist, and turned her hand over to examine her bloody palm.

"What happened to you, crazy girl?" he asked in the voice of a concerned father. "Did you fall?"

"Not exactly," she said.

"It was that bad man."

Both adults lowered their eyes to the child behind the counter. The pencil in his hand was still poised over his notebook, but his eyes were on Rachel, his expression cool but firm, as if he were a teacher trying to impart a simple truth to his student.

Mr. El Sayed frowned a little at his son. "Naji," he scolded. "Do not interrupt."

"It was that bad man," the boy repeated, never taking his eyes off Rachel. "The man who bought the juice. He's done bad things."

"Why would you say that?" the father pressed.

"He's all empty inside," Naji said, his voice trembling just a bit. "There's no light inside him. He scares me."

"Me too," Rachel agreed, looking at her palms.

Mr. El Sayed squinted curiously at her, at his son, and then at her again. "Why did you chase that man?" he finally asked.

"You'll save us both a headache if you don't ask," she said.

He nodded solemnly and accepted her card, but then, instead of swiping it, he set it on the counter and walked away. Rachel watched him, too tired to be too curious, as he walked down one of the aisles. He returned a moment later with gauze and bandages. He put them in the bag with the soda, buns, and cheese. She started to protest, but he silenced her with a wave.

"No charge," he said. "You returned as you promised."

As much as she disliked taking anything she hadn't earned, Rachel didn't have the strength to argue. She smiled gratefully at Mr. El Sayed. "Thank you, sir," she said. "You have a good heart."

The compliment softened his expression and brought out a seldom-seen smile that warmed Rachel's weary soul. "Take better care of yourself, crazy girl," he said. "For your grandfather's sake."

BACK AT THE house, Rachel changed her clothes and cleaned and dressed her wounds while her laptop scanned the files on the USB key for viruses. Finding none, it loaded the flash drive's contents onto the screen. It was stuffed to the brim with large files—a mix of scanned items and typed documents, each of them potentially a case-breaker for her.

She clicked on the first file, eager for a clue that would salvage her pride. But she couldn't read it. The language in the document was one she couldn't even identify, and her computer didn't recognize it either. She opened the next file only to discover a different language, also unfamiliar. The third document was composed of some sort of hieroglyphics, and the fourth was written in an alphabet she had never seen before. Growing increasingly perplexed, she opened one file after another.

Twenty minutes later, she slammed her bandaged hands on the tabletop and shrieked a curse. She couldn't read them! Hundreds of documents, and she couldn't read a single one.

While in training for her job as a daemon collector, she'd been required to learn at least two languages currently in use in the Notan world. Though it wasn't explicitly stated anywhere in the training materials, it was well-known among trainees that the more common the languages the collector knew, the better the assignments she would get. Granted, there had to be a few people on staff who spoke those obscure languages that only a few hundred people had even heard of, but the best chance of traveling to a wide variety of places was to speak a major Notan language. Currently, Rachel was fluent in five languages (English, German, Spanish, Common Arcanan, and K'Maz, her mother's native tongue), and she knew a smattering of several others on top of that, but none of that was proving to be of any help with what she'd found on the flash drive.

Her bruised ego suffered another blow as she finally admitted to herself that she wasn't going to be able to fix this mess alone.

Snarling quietly, she picked up her phone and called the local office. Generally speaking, collectors weren't supposed to punt their cases back to the Skiptrace office, but in this case her request was appropriate. As things stood, she could not continue work on this job until she knew what was on this damn memory stick, and she wasn't going to figure it out by staring at the computer screen until she was cross-eyed. She hoped that someone in the office would either know the languages she needed or would know how to get the documents translated. Then maybe she could get back on track.

The phone rang. And rang. And rang.

After fifteen rings, Rachel hung up—annoyed and agitated, but mostly confused. The office never closed. Daemon monitoring was a twenty-four-hour operation; someone was always, always at the desk.

She continued to click through files while calling every number she had for the Daemonic Monitoring Department. After an hour of placing unanswered calls, her frustration was boiling out of control. She let her last phone call ring thirty times before finally punching the end button, slamming her laptop shut, and screaming aloud. Still confused but now also thoroughly pissed, she put on her coat, pocketed the USB key, and headed out her door. If she couldn't get the office on the phone, she would go there in person.

THE OFFICE WAS sealed.

When she tried to walk through the shadowy space between the old door and the restaurant wall, she was met with a cold, solid wall. She'd been cut off from the Skiptrace office. After bumping her nose, she cursed, kicked the door, and shrieked for someone to let her in. A few restaurant employees who were loitering out back stared at her nervously. One of them whispered something to his companion in Greek.

Though she didn't speak the language, one of the words got her attention; it was almost identical to the word her mother used when her brother started commanding the sheep to dance for him after chugging a bottle of wine at the harvest celebration.

Angry but determined not to draw undue attention, Rachel shoved her hands in her pockets and left.

She wasn't sure how to handle this. She wandered around the area for a while, calling the office again and again, but the result was always the same: it rang continuously for two minutes straight, and then the call was unceremoniously cut off. She couldn't even leave a message.

Baffled, she tried calling a few friends and colleagues. No one was able to offer her any insight.

Every call Rachel made pissed her off more and more, until her cell phone was shaking in her clenched fingers. The office never closed! That doorway had never been shut, never! And why wasn't anyone answering the phone? She balled her fists and pinched her lips tight to muffle the roar in her throat. Her whole body shook and her teeth ground together as her repressed rage burst from her core and exploded through every pore. With great effort, she kept her fury silent until she regained control and her irate tremors ceased. As her body stilled, she stowed her anger in a corner of her mind and made herself a promise that she would unleash it on the first person from the Skiptrace office she actually managed to speak to.

She decided to head back to her house. It was either that or find a place nearby to wait until the passage reopened, and she was in no mood to be in public. She felt the need to scream and curse, preferably in her native tongue, and she couldn't do that where Notans could see her.

As she turned on her heel to head back the way she'd come, she collided with a man who was walking up behind her.

"Sorry," she mumbled. "Excuse me."

"No," he said. He grabbed her by the elbow. "Um, no."

Startled, she glanced up at him. He was a young man, in his early twenties, but he had the sunken eyes of a much older man. He was shuffling his weight from foot to foot, unable to stay still for even a second, and his bloodshot eyes twitched wildly. A whiff of chemicals and rot floated about him.

Rachel wrinkled her nose, yanked her arm free, and tried to move around the man, but he stepped into her path.

"Back off," she snapped.

"Give me your money."

She stepped around him and started walking away.

He grabbed her elbow and tugged her back. "Give me your money," he repeated quietly.

"Get bent," she said.

He tried to reach his hand into her coat pocket, but she smacked it away and shoved him in the chest. He stumbled backward a few steps, caught himself before tripping, reversed his trajectory, and lunged at her.

Relieved to have an outlet for her frustration, Rachel pulled back and slapped the guy as hard as she could. A satisfying tingle vibrated through her bandaged hand.

The violence of the contact clearly rattled him—his wide eyes blinked rapidly and his mouth fell open—but not enough to send him running. Instead, he pulled a knife out of his pocket and waved it in her direction. "Give me your money, bitch!"

"I am so freakin' tired of people who are trying to hurt me calling me a bitch," she said. "Get outta my face and go fuck yourself!"

Twitching like a cricket on a hot plate, he made a few half-hearted jabs in her direction, but they grew weaker when she folded her arms over her chest and stared at him without moving. They grew even more timid as she continued to stare him down. It wasn't long before he started to inch his way backward, edging away from her. After casting one last sneer at him, Rachel confidently turned her back.

Half a second later, Rachel heard the mugger coming at her again. She calmly stepped out of the way. He barreled right past her, teetering on his unsteady legs, then whirled around, swinging his pocket knife in a wide, pointless arc, and tried to grab her arm again.

"Just walk away," she said, smoothly moving out of his reach. "Don't make me kick your useless ass."

"Give me your money!"

He lunged again and this time, without hesitation, she punched him in the face. Short and small though she was, she was plenty capable of inflicting damage on a twitchy man whose only hand-to-hand combat experience probably came from video games.

Reeling from the blow, the mugger dropped his knife and grabbed his face with both hands. Blood dripped through his fingers. "Bitch!" he shouted through his hands.

"Whatever," she said.

He threw out an arm and swiped at her blindly. She side-stepped his shaking fingers and tried to walk away, but he made one last attempt to grab her. As his knuckles brushed her arm, Rachel drew back her fist to land a second punch, but before she could take her shot, a blur of blue whooshed across her vision and slammed into the mugger, flattening him against a wall.

"It was her!" the attacker shrieked. "She—"

"You tried to mug her and got what was coming to you," said the blur. "Fuck off already."

"No! I—"

"It's not her fault your girlfriend ran off with your money," said the stranger. "If you need to steal to get your next fix, then go steal from your clueless grandmother. That poor woman still thinks you're in school. Go see her before your parents give up hope and stop shielding her from the truth."

Stunned, bleeding, and entirely out of willpower, the would-be mugger slunk away. Rachel barely noticed his departure. Her attention was filled by the strange man who had appeared out of nowhere. Clothed in a blue hospital gown and a baggy old coat, he was filthy, scruffy, and dragging the tube for an IV bag from his sleeve.

She squinted at him and cocked her head, as if seeing him from a different angle might make his presence more logical. "Mr. Oracle?" she whispered.

"Hey." He turned to look at her, and for the first time she saw clarity in his electric-blue eyes. "Good to see you."

"What hap—I mean, are you okay?"

"Oh yeah." He laughed gently. "Yeah, I'm great. I haven't felt this good in a long damn time. And I kinda feel like . . ." He stared at her with a strange intensity. "Like maybe I need to talk to you."

BACH

"Are you sure it's okay?"

Rachel stopped and glanced over her shoulder. They were only a few steps away from the passage that led to her house, and the oracle was eyeing the shadow like it might be full of scorpions.

"It's fine," she insisted for the third time. "I walk through it every day."

"But I can't see it."

"You aren't supposed to. That's how it stays hidden."

He didn't look convinced, so she tried to work a little assurance into her voice.

"Relax. It's easy."

"You won't get in trouble?"

"No," she lied. "It's fine. Now come on, let's go."

He took a deep breath and followed on her heels as she stepped into the inkblot shadow and crossed into the pocket dimension. Rachel lost all sense of him while in the passage, just as she lost all sense of everything, but moments after she exited, she felt his presence again.

A SHIVER WENT through Bach as he stepped over the threshold and onto her front walk. He closed his eyes and shook his head to dispel the extraordinary disquiet he had experienced in the dark. Then, forcing his eyes to open, he looked at his new surroundings. The house at the end of the walk was run-down but ordinary enough, and the sky beyond it looked appropriately blue. When his gaze slid to the right, however, his sense of perception was jolted. The lawn that surrounded the house bled into the sky in a colorful smear just a short stretch from where he stood. He followed the blue upward until his nose was pointed straight above him. The sky up there was blue, but the color was mist-like and insubstantial. Beyond the mist, where the sky should stretch into infinity, there was nothing but a white expanse, as though the house and its lawn were encased in a canvas sphere. It was as though he had entered a painting that was bounded by a dome-shaped frame. It was both mesmerizing and hard to look at.

"What happens if you go to the edge?" he asked.

"I don't know," the girl said. "I haven't tried. But I wouldn't recommend it. It could be that you'd walk into a solid wall where the dimension ends, but it's equally likely that you'd fall off the edge and disappear."

Disappear. The word was like a cold breath down his back. "That's a little creepy," he muttered.

"Says the guy who lives under a bridge."

"Hey, the bridge thing is a relatively new development in my life," he said. "I've only been there for"—he calculated in his head—"about six months. Before that, I had an apartment."

"So what happened?"

"I lost control of my . . . what did you call it? My sight-beyond?"

"Yes." She pursed her lips. "There's an actual word for it in my language, but it doesn't translate well. 'Sight-beyond' is pretty close."

"Whatever you call it, it got the better of me. Something in my head kinda popped, and suddenly I couldn't keep it together anymore. The last six months have been a mess. I only remember bits and pieces."

They climbed the front steps and walked through the unlocked door into the foyer.

The girl stopped inside the door to remove her coat. "So what changed?"

"I dunno," he said. "I remember picking up that thing on the ground and feeling a shock go through me."

"You had a seizure."

"Seizure?" he asked in surprise. "That's different. Anyway, when I woke up, I was in the hospital, and it was like I was back inside in my head after months of being off in Nowheresville. I feel like myself again. Well"—he plucked at his grimy beard—"not exactly like myself. I hate to ask, but could I take a shower?"

"I don't mind." She waved a hand toward the staircase nearby. "There's a bathroom upstairs on the left. Oh, and there are some men's clothes in one of the bedrooms. The last collector to use this house must have left them behind. If something fits, take it."

"Awesome. Thanks."

He eagerly climbed the stairs, stripping off his layers as he went. As he stepped into the bathroom, he removed the remnants of the IV from his arm; then he started fumbling with the controls on the shower, already shivering in the cool air.

What he saw in the bathroom was unlike anything he was accustomed to. There were buttons and switches in strange places, some of them with peculiar lettering, and there were pipes, faucets, and porcelain in shapes he didn't recognize. There was a bathtub of sorts, but it was barely half the size of any bathtub he'd ever seen, and the shower stall had not one but two nozzles—the first in the traditional place, the second located at roughly waist level and poised above a small basin that jutted out of the shower wall. There was no sink, only a strange slot in the vanity countertop that glowed and hummed when he stuck his hands into it. The toilet had no tank on it and no water in the bowl (suddenly, he was grateful that he had used the facilities in the hospital before leaving).

After a few minutes of trial and error, he managed to get the shower working. The water was lukewarm, at best, but it was clean and clear. He stepped into the shower stall and stood under the nozzle.

The water struck his body at once but did not immediately reach him; it took many long seconds before enough grime was washed away to expose his bare skin. He reached for a bar of soap that was resting on the edge of the shower basin. It felt rough, almost like a solidified chunk of sand, but when he rubbed it between his hands, the dirt that seemed like it might be permanently caked on them came loose. The soap didn't become sudsy, as he expected it would, but it did give off a clean odor—something reminiscent of lawn clippings.

More and more of his body appeared from beneath the grime. He took a breath so deep that his lungs strained to contain it. He had not had a shower in six months. Six months of dirt and filth from the ground he'd slept on. Six months of sweat, saliva, and vomit, most but not all of it his own. Six months of dried blood from injuries received from people who'd hit him to steal what little he had or to shut him up when his ramblings frightened them. Six months of smearing rancid garbage on his hands and face as he rummaged through the trash cans of the living. Six months of urine and fecal matter from the times when he was too far gone in his delusions to remember that he had a body to care for. Six months. And now it was being washed away like it was nothing but simple dirt. The filth, the fluids, the unholy stink—he felt like the clock was spinning backward, returning his lost time and resetting his life to the point before he had let it slip away.

He had forgotten many long months ago that there was a man underneath the mess, but now he could feel that person surfacing again. He was still human. He was still alive. Tears welled up in his bloodshot eyes and rolled down his face amidst quiet sobs.

RACHEL WENT TO the living room and plopped down on the couch. She rubbed her eyes and took a deep breath. She had broken the number one rule of her job, the rule that applied to everyone from her homeland: do not introduce people from the Nota to the Arcana. It sometimes happened that people from the Nota accidentally stumbled into the Arcana, but it was never, ever supposed to happen by Arcanan initiative. She was definitely going to get her ears chewed off for this.

Technically, though, this oracle, using his special ability, had inserted himself into her life without her help—a fact she would be sure to cite when her superiors were reaming her for this. Sight-beyond gave oracles access to all sorts of information that they had no ordinary means of learning. It flowed into their brains, unbidden, and waited there, snuggled into random recesses, until the oracle either called it up or stumbled upon it. Oracles who resisted the flow generally started to lose control of their minds as the extrasensory data built up and cluttered their brains.

Despite having lost six months of his life, this man seemed to be handling the flow remarkably well. Even if she had tried to avoid getting entangled in his life, he could have found his way back to her. Put all together, it seemed like a very gray area to her.

Not that the Central Office would see it that way.

Feeling weary, she turned on the wall screen and scrolled through the options in the main menu. From the master list, she clicked first on "Northern Arcanum," then "Plains Region," then "Kritt," and then scrolled down the list of clan names for her own: Wilde. It was the end of the harvest season and everyone was busy bringing in the crop, but there were a few recent updates to the public record. Her grandfather had undergone another treatment for his bad leg. Her sister had briefly been allowed to visit the family.

Rachel felt a pang to think that she had not been home to see her. It could be months or even years before Caras was well enough for another visit.

Near the bottom of the page, she saw that her big brother had been ejected from yet another Kritt Council meeting for foul language. Underneath that posting, there was an additional message addressed to Rachel's mother from the Council Speaker: *Elafina—kindly teach your son to hold his tongue and digest the words a woman speaks to him, as is proper behavior for a man.*

Below that was a response from her mother: *I taught him to digest wisdom and never to swallow shit. Which did you attempt to feed him, Saviza?*

Rachel snickered and jutted out her chin with daughterly pride. There was a personal message for her, which she was thrilled to receive. Written by her grandfather, the message included lots of photographs of her little nephew. Rachel grinned. He was so cute! He had always looked so much like his mother, Rettie, but the older he got, the more his smile reminded Rachel of the boy's father—her little brother, Wilham.

She moved closer to the screen to read her grandfather's message:

My girl,

There has been plenty to keep our hands busy while you've been away. We celebrated Hart's first birthday. We seated Rettie, the mother of the day, at the head of the table and toasted her before the meal, offering her our thanks and respect. The menu she chose for the evening was unusual, being largely dishes that she grew up with and not things you would find around here, but we enjoyed it. Your aunt made Hart a fruit tart with a custard filling. He seemed suspicious of it at first, but once he had a taste, he tried to stuff the entire thing in his mouth. Quite a mess he made! I've sent you a picture. Just look at that grin.

The autumn storms have been especially harsh this year. There was a freak lightning strike at the Sokol clan's barn that burned down most of the roof. Your parents and brothers helped to haul away the charred timbers and rebuild the barn. I offered to help, but your aunt insisted that I stay off my feet. My bad knee is making an invalid of me.

Rettie is fitting in well in Kritt. She's got a natural

patience that makes her well suited to work in daemon collection items. She's made some exceptional gloves, even better than the ones you use, and next month she learns to make perception-shifting glasses. Daemon Collection Services is impressed with her work. Our neighbors have had nothing but positive things to say about her, both her personally and her work. Macci Saviza doesn't care much for her, but, in my opinion, that speaks highly of Rettie. I look forward to next season when the Kash matriarch replaces that woman as Council Speaker.

Rachel flinched to see Dhruv's clan name, and was grateful that her grandfather hadn't mentioned the breakup. Her parents, who had sent her the last message she'd received from home, had not shown the same sensitivity.

The rest of the message was pretty standard: *busy harvesting . . . good crop this year . . . sheep are healthy . . . new dog herding well . . . chickens laying eggs.* And there at the end was the blurb she loved seeing the most: *We miss you, my girl. We love you. I love you. Come home as soon as possible.*

She smiled. She loved hearing from home, but she had the feeling that such a long message meant that her poor grandfather was bored out of his skull. His bad leg often kept him from working, and he hated being idle. He was probably driving her aunt crazy being in the house all day. If Rachel closed her eyes, she could hear the old man cursing like a one-eyed carpenter as he hobbled from room to room while her aunt barked at him to sit down.

She smiled wistfully. Homesickness was turning her into a daydreamer.

WHEN HE FIRST emerged from the shower stall, Bach's heart almost exploded with shock to see a strange man in the room with him.

A moment later, his pulse slowed as he realized what he was seeing was actually his reflection. He approached the mirror slowly, half-afraid to look at himself. It was definitely his face in that mirror, though he hardly recognized it. His beard and hair were clean now, but they were grown out long—entirely unlike his usual appearance. His skin, usually pale but clear, was weather-beaten and scored with injuries. He glanced around the bathroom and poked through the drawers and cabinets until he found some cuticle scissors and a straight razor. Cutting his hair with the little scissors was a painfully slow process, but it yielded positive results. In the absence of shaving cream, he did his best to lather his face with the bar soap before picking up the razor. He got a few nicks, but as his skin was already marred with cuts and bruises, they blended in well.

His work done, he splashed water on his face and rubbed his cheeks and chin with a towel. His reflection, familiar at last, gazed back at him in wonder and relief.

The nearest tiny bedroom's even tinier closet revealed a very small selection of men's clothes. A white button-down shirt and an old pair of jeans looked like they might fit, but once on his body, they hung from his underfed frame like drapes from a curtain rod. He tucked the shirt into the jeans, which he tightened around his waist with tied-together shoelaces from the only pair of shoes in the closet (which were too small for his feet).

Barefoot, he descended the stairs and stepped into the living room. The girl sat on the couch with her back to him. His "sight-beyond" told him she had violated some very important rules to give him this second chance at humanity, and that made him all the more grateful to her. He promised himself—promised on the Bible, promised on his grandmother's grave, promised on his life—he would make it up to her somehow.

No sooner had he made this promise than his sight-beyond told him, vaguely but undoubtedly, that repaying this debt was going to cost him dearly. *That's okay*, he told himself confidently. *Whatever the cost, I'll pay it.*

"I can't thank you enough," he said. "You can never know what this means to me."

She glanced over her shoulder at him and started in surprise. Bach drew back a bit, confused and worried, but then a yip of laughter sprang from her lips.

"You're blond!" she said.

"What?"

She closed her eyes and shook her head, still laughing quietly. "You're blond!" she said again, gesturing toward his head. "Under all that dirt, you were blond!"

"Oh." He chuckled and ran one hand through his sunny hair. "Yeah. Surprise."

Her bright brown eyes took in his new appearance very thoroughly. From the expression on her face, he understood how different he now looked. His scraggly hair was gone, cut short. He still had cuts and bruises, some of them pretty unsightly, but the clothes concealed most of them and the shower had removed the caked-on dirt that accentuated them. His skin was sun-damaged but noticeably pale now that the layer of filth that had previously coated it was gone. There was a change in her expression, a shift in her level of respect (she would never call him "mister" again, that was obvious), that told him she had just realized for the first time that he was younger than her.

While she appraised him, he looked at her closely for the first time. She was young but a few years older than him; the extra years showed in the forward way she carried herself and the confidence in her bearing. Though she was small, both short and compact, now that he saw her without her coat on, he could see that she was a bit thicker around the middle than he'd supposed. This was the figure of a farm girl, he realized, who had been raised on breakfasts of eggs and bacon. Her thick torso, along with her limbs, had been hardened into muscle by twenty-odd years of daily farm labor. What he had initially taken for a light suntan, he now recognized as the natural tint of her skin, and she had a certain slant to her face that hinted at a mixed heritage. Bits of her personal history popped into his mind, and he tucked the information away for future consideration.

"What's your name?" she asked.

"Bach."

"Is that your first or last name?"

"Yeah."

He stepped around her with hardly a glance at her puzzled expression and walked up to the screen on the wall. Some sort of message was pulled up on the display, along with photos of a little boy.

Bach squinted at the foreign words on the screen. "What language is this?"

"Common Arcanan. It's my native tongue."

"What's with this television?"

"It's not a television," she told him. "It's an in-home utility screen. It controls pretty much everything in this house—water, lights, locks, windows, everything."

"Amazing."

"Not really." She shrugged. "No one back home uses these. My people only install obsolete technology like this in temporary housing. The utility system in my family's home is much better. Still," she admitted, "this one has some good features. It can pick up television and radio broadcasts from the Nota—that's the world where you're from—and it can pick up a variety of broadcasts from the Arcana, where I'm from."

"Which is in another dimension."

"It's at another level in the human dimensional spectrum, yes."

"How many levels are there?"

"In this spectrum? Seven."

"There are seven dimensions with people in them?" he said excitedly. "Really?"

"No, there are only people in four of them."

"But . . . never mind." He laughed. "I think I'm in over my head. But you . . . catch demons. It's your job to catch demons that aren't . . . functioning properly." He cocked his head curiously, surprised to hear himself speak such words. "Is that right?" he asked her. "Demons break down and need to be fixed, just like old cars? That's awesome!"

"It's not as glamorous as it sounds," she said. "I pick up daemons that aren't doing what they're supposed to do, and I bring them in for correction. That's all."

"How are they corrected?"

"I don't really know. That's not my department."

"But your whole society, your whole dimension, is built around making sure demons keep doing what they're supposed to do?"

"Basically." She narrowed her eyes at him, a gesture neither malicious nor worried but merely curious. "How much do you know about me?"

"I really don't know," he admitted with half a laugh. "The first time I saw you, I got a massive dose of information, but I'm just now starting to sort it out. New stuff keeps popping up. For instance, this kid"—he pointed to the photos on the screen—"is your nephew. He's cute. What's his name?"

"Hart."

"And he's the son of your younger brother and his . . . wife? Are they married?"

"Um . . ." She seemed to be searching for the correct answer. "No, not the way you mean. They live together in my family's home and they raise their son together, but no, they didn't make a religious-based commitment."

"You have another brother," Bach marched on. "Older than you. And you have a younger sister."

"Grigor and Caras," she told him. Her face tightened when she spoke her sister's name. "I'd rather not—"

"Your sister," he rambled on, "she's very sweet but she's got some kind of . . . oh."

Too late, he realized he had erred. He glanced at his hostess's reflection in the screen and saw how her features had hardened. Guilt coiled in his stomach. The exact nature of her sister's condition or illness was not clear to him, but he sensed that it was severely disabling, ultimately fatal, and a source of quiet but continuous sorrow for his new friend. This wasn't the first time in his life he had let his sight-beyond run his mouth, but under the circumstances, he felt a crushing remorse. He hadn't intended to poke a wound.

A tense pause hung in the air, during which Bach couldn't bring himself to turn around and meet her eyes. Determined to change the subject, he scanned the screen again, his eyes rapidly searching for any little item that might draw up a stored memory.

"This," he said, pointing to a word, "is your name. Wilde. You're . . . Rachel. Rachel Wilde. Am I right?"

The tension left her face, though she continued to watch him carefully. "That's me," she confirmed. "Except that's not how my name is pronounced in the Arcana."

He blinked and cocked his head. "There's another way to pronounce 'Rachel'?"

"There's no *cha* sound in my native language," she said. "In Arcanan, when the letters *C* and *H* are together, they're pronounced like a *K*. So 'Rachel,' in my language, is pronounced 'Rah-kel.'"

He smiled. "So how would you introduce yourself?"

"Wilde Rachel len Wilde. In your language that would translate to 'Rachel Wilde of Clan Wilde.'"

"That's a mouthful. Can I call you Rae?" He grinned at her.

After a brief pause, she returned his smile. "No one calls me that. But my brothers call me Ra. So, anything else about me you already know?"

"That's all I'm getting right now."

"Hmm." She gave a sharp nod. "It's not as much as I thought it would be."

"What do you mean?"

"Considering how long you've been following me around, I assumed you would have picked up more."

"Following you?" He frowned as he searched his spotty memory. "I remember seeing you several times but . . . sorry, I don't know why I followed you. Maybe it was just part of my delusions. Or maybe I had a legitimate reason that I can't remember anymore. Or maybe," he said with a grateful smile, "my sight-beyond told me that I had to be near you to snap out of the crazies."

Rachel nodded, shrugged, and gestured toward the sofa. Bach followed her lead and sat down next to her, carefully maintaining a certain distance. He didn't want to make her uncomfortable.

"So what's your story?" she asked. "Why the bridge?"

"It's . . . complicated," he said hesitantly. "I've had this sight-beyond thing as long as I can remember, but it never caused much trouble until six months ago."

"What happened then?"

"I had a bunch of things happen at once. I was finishing up school, I was looking for a job, I went through an ugly breakup, I had an epic fight with my family . . . and one night I woke up from a deep sleep suddenly knowing for sure that something huge was right on the horizon. I struggled to keep it all together, and I was handling it for a while but . . . it was so much stress." He groaned as the memories flooded back. "All this daily life crap came at me at once, and all the while my sight-beyond is in high gear for some reason, and one day it . . . it was just too much. Something in my head snapped. I couldn't keep my mind in order anymore, and reality kinda walked away from me." He looked at her and shook his head. "I can't say it any better than that."

She tilted her head and tightened her lips. He sensed that his explanation was not entirely satisfying to her but that she didn't feel comfortable quizzing him. That wasn't surprising. This was really the first time they had met, when it came down to it, and she wouldn't want to ask too many personal questions of a stranger. Besides, she had work to do. That was where her thoughts were focused. That was why she had sought him out.

"Will you do something for me?" she asked.

"If I can."

She fished something out of her pocket and held it up before his face. A flash drive. Sparks flared inside him as he looked at it.

"There's a familiar sight," he said.

"Any chance you could tell me where to find its owner? Or what's on it?"

"Can't you hook it up to this thing"—he jerked his thumb toward the wall screen—"or that laptop I saw in the other room?"

"I tried but I can't read the languages on it. I wanted to take it into the . . . to where I work for help, but for some reason the office is closed. Listen," she said, her tone level and serious, "even overlooking for the moment that I have a job to do, the guy who dropped this is very dangerous. I need to find him, fast, and this thing is the only link I have to him. I sent samples of the documents on this thing to several people I know—mostly daemon collectors like me—but so far no one's been helpful. I don't like to do this, but the local office hasn't left me much choice. I think I have to use an expert from the Nota to read this stuff. But the thing is, if I go to a Notan who asks a lot of questions about me or how I got this memory stick, I'm fucked. I don't expect you to be able to translate all this stuff, but I thought maybe you could point me in the direction of someone who can help while not being too nosy." She smiled hopefully and offered him the USB key. "What d'ya say?"

"I say I owe you big and I'll do anything you'd like me to

do," he replied, plucking the drive from her fingers. "Let's see if I get anything from your little clue here."

He held it in between his right thumb and forefinger and looked at it closely. On its surface, it was unremarkable. Its body was gray and black, sleek and glossy. There was a mark of some kind on its back, some sort of tiny logo, but he didn't recognize the brand. There was a dent, probably from when it was dropped during the scuffle, and a scratch on one end that suggested it had once been attached to something. Bach felt his sight-beyond kick out some information, but when he reviewed it, he was disappointed.

"Your guy used to have this thing clipped on his keychain," he said. "He was so paranoid about losing it that he didn't want it out of his sight. The keychain broke when you knocked his keys out of his pocket. He grabbed the keys after fighting you, but he didn't see that the flash drive was gone."

"Anything else?"

"Just a feeling that he's a tough customer." He flashed her an apologetic expression and handed her the drive. "Sorry."

"It's okay. Thanks for trying." She picked up the remote on the coffee table, pointed it at the wall, and started clicking through menu options. "I'll just have to pick some expert at random and hope for the best."

Local listings appeared on the large screen. Fascinated, Bach absorbed the display of unfamiliar technology as Rachel calmly flipped through several categories before finding a list of language consultants.

"The problem here," she said under her breath, "is that I don't know what languages I'm dealing with. It's going to be a little weird to walk into someone's office and try to explain why I have a memory stick full of foreign-language documents

if I don't even know what languages those documents are written in." She stared at the long list of names, her nostrils flared.
"How do I know who to see?"

"You're in the wrong category."

Rachel turned to him, eyebrows raised. He felt an equally
surprised expression overtake his own face.

"What's that?" she asked.

"Wrong category," he repeated, marveling at the words
coming unbidden from his mouth. "Oh, I know something," he
murmured thoughtfully. "Give me a second." His eyes vibrated
as their gaze turned inward, seeking out the information that
was gently prodding him from the crevasses of his mind. "You
want a category called 'Museums.'"

He could feel her watching him as he stared straight ahead,
his eyes not seeing what was before him, his attention focused
inward. He heard a few clicks, and then Rachel prompted him.

"Now what?"

"There should be a list of employee names for the
Rigaceen Museum of Natural and Human History."

She clicked again. "There it is."

His eyes gradually refocused. He stood up and walked
closer to the screen, his eyes dancing over the list of names.
He slowly ran his forefinger down the column. "Swan," he
mumbled. "Swan, swan, swan . . ."

His finger slowed and hovered over the name "Dr. H.
Swann." But no, that wasn't it. He pointed farther down the list
to a name near the bottom. "That's your expert," he said decisively. "No doubt about it."

Rachel clicked on the name. Bach watched as she squinted at
the brief biography pulled up from the museum website, and saw
her sag a little. Clearly, the profile struck her as unimpressive.

"Are you sure?" she asked. "This says she's an assistant to the museum curator. Doesn't say a thing about language expertise."

"Trust me," he said. "She's the one you're looking for." He could feel it.

Rachel wrinkled her nose a bit and glanced over the biography again. "What about all that babble about a swan?" she ventured. "Are you sure I shouldn't call this Dr. Swann?"

"That threw me at first, too," he said. "But check out the assistant's name." He pointed at it. "Leda Morley," he read. "Leda, like the Greek queen who was seduced by a god in the form of a swan." Bach chuckled humorlessly and pointed at his head. "It's weird how things get bounced around up here. Sometimes I don't know what I know until it comes out of my mouth."

Rachel looked again and nodded with a comprehending sigh. "But you're sure she's the right person for this?"

"As sure as I've ever been."

An uncertain sound rumbled in Rachel's throat. She looked sidelong at the screen, as if it was a platter of food that smelled appetizing despite having an off-putting appearance.

"Okay," she finally said. "I'll give her a call. But"—and here her tone grew sharp—"if things go squirrelly, I'm taking it out on you."

"It'll be fine," he said.

He spoke with a confidence he didn't quite feel. Miss Morley was indisputably the right person for the job, and yet there was a doubt in the back of his mind—a tiny doubt, just a speck, but it was persistently present, like a grain of sand caught between two toes. What was it?

When the answer didn't immediately come forward, he

decided to ignore the misgiving and give Miss Morley his wholehearted recommendation. This woman had returned his humanity to him and he was eager to repay her.

He nodded smartly. "Nothing to worry about."

After a moment's hesitation, Rachel pulled out her phone.

EXPERT

The Rigaceen was an immense complex surrounded by greenery that enclosed the building like a moat, providing a small degree of separation from the busy streets. It was a formidable structure, a fortress of solid gray that rose three stories tall and stretched to fill most of a city block. Multistory banners hung on the front face of the museum, advertising new exhibits, while smaller banners, frayed and faded, stood near the doors to remind visitors of older displays still available for viewing. Two realistic-looking dinosaur statues flanked the front steps, a triceratops and velociraptor, though the snarling predator was made considerably less fearsome by the colorful tie around its neck and the beer bottle in its three-fingered hand (the late-night contribution of a drunken pedestrian, Rachel guessed).

Just inside the doors, above the information desk, an enormous photo of the Rigaceen family, the patrons of the museum, smiled benevolently through a printed statement welcoming visitors to their generous endowment. Rachel rolled her eyes at the picture. Those people gave off the air of royalty bestowing a favor on the little people. History wasn't to be owned and handed out like trinkets. It certainly shouldn't be attached to one family's name. That, she felt, was the absolute personification of arrogance and elitism. She wrinkled her nose, recalling a lesson from childhood: *There is no surer sign of a diseased culture than the casual acceptance of inequities.*

The receptionist got on her phone to confirm Rachel's appointment with Miss Morley and then kindly provided directions through the maze of hallways by taking out a visitor's map and marking the way with her pen.

Rachel passed through a few exhibitions on her way to the employee wing, and as she did, she reflected that she rarely got a chance to visit places like this back home anymore. Between work on her family's farm and daemon collecting, her time had seldom been her own ever since leaving school. But as a child, she had really enjoyed museums and historical sites.

Her eyes drifted over the artifacts and displays, and she felt a nostalgic buzz of curiosity. It was a shame, she thought, that the Central Office wouldn't sanction spending money on nonnecessities, or she would come back sometime and spend a leisurely day wandering the halls. *Honestly, charging people money to gain access to their own history. What a disgrace!*

Pushing aside her loathing, she made a note to check the website just in case the museum offered a free day. It would be nice to lose herself in history for a while, even if it was just Notan history.

The assistant to the curator had a small, cluttered office. Boxes were stacked four feet high against the far wall, though the stacks were left lower in one area to allow sunlight from the window to pierce the encroaching shadows. Dark though the room was, Rachel preferred it to the fluorescent-lit hallways she had navigated to find this office; fluorescents gave her terrible eyestrain.

Behind the desk, several framed degrees and photographs were hung in such a way as to accommodate the twin filing cabinets that towered over all like a pair of metal giants. The musky scent of the museum wafted by the door in gusts, but inside the office it was muted by a floral aroma, either perfume or a scented candle. It all smelled artificial and stuffy to Rachel, who wished she could open the window to let in the clean scent of autumn air.

When the office's occupant spotted her at the door, she rose from her desk with a smile and offered her hand in greeting. "Miss Wilde? Leda Morley. Nice to meet you."

"You too," said Rachel, shaking her hand. "Thanks for meeting with me today."

"Not at all. Please, have a seat."

Though Rachel was still reluctant to hand the flash drive to Miss Morley, Bach's certainty, combined with the fact that she still could not reach her superiors, had convinced her that this was the best thing to do. So she told Miss Morley a made-up story about how she'd come to possess the memory stick and asked if she could possibly translate any of it for her, just to satisfy her curiosity.

The curator's assistant seemed happy to comply, so Rachel sat on the far side of the woman's desk and waited with fake patience while she loaded the files.

Leda Morley was a young woman, only a few years older than Rachel. She was dressed in a frilly blue skirt and white knit top, which were pleasantly muted by a dark blue blazer. She wore well-coordinated jewelry and pumps with intimidating heels. She had the long, tapered fingers of a lady-in-waiting and the buffered expression of a woman intent on climbing a career ladder. Her black hair was styled perfectly straight, and her light dusting of makeup was nicely complimentary to her features. Rachel found the Notan obsession with professional appearance to be nonsensical—dressing in restrictive clothing too expensive to risk damaging struck her as an impediment to a hard day's work—but the way Miss Morley presented herself strongly suggested that she took her job seriously, and that gave Rachel confidence.

Over the next few minutes, Miss Morley's dark, dark eyes danced over her computer screen, and occasionally darted in Rachel's direction, with a light of scientific fascination in their depths.

"This is very interesting stuff," she finally said, nodding at the computer. Her voice was rich, like coffee, but had a measured quality to it, as though she was accustomed to choosing her words with care. "Where did you say you got it?"

"My great-uncle died recently," Rachel lied. "This thing was in the stuff I got from his estate."

"Was he a historian or archaeologist?"

"I don't think so."

Miss Morley's contoured eyebrows twitched slightly and her thick lips pursed. "You don't think so?"

"I didn't know much about him," Rachel said, trying to sound casual. "He was kind of the black sheep of the family. As far as I know, nobody from my family had talked to him in ten years or so. If you can read what's on those files, then you probably know more about him than I do." She cocked her head and smiled in what she hoped was a not-too-eager sort of way. "*Can* you read it?"

"Sort of," Miss Morley said. "This is some sort of cursive variant of Middle Egyptian, but it seems to be an obscure dialect that I'm unfamiliar with. It'll take some time to translate."

She clicked the mouse and continued to stare at the screen. "This could be Turkish. If it is, I'd guess it's Ottoman Turkish. That won't be too difficult." She clicked again, her interest blazing through her eyes. "These are the real mystery." She leaned forward in her chair, the light of the screen reflecting in her eyes. "At first glance, this one looks like some variant of Central Semitic. Could be Phoenician . . . maybe Punic. This other one . . . I have no idea."

"I'm sorry," Rachel politely interrupted. "I don't follow you at all."

"Oh!" Miss Morley blinked rapidly, seemingly surprised to realize that Rachel was still in her office. She straightened up and smiled kindly. "I'm sorry! These files of yours are just very interesting. With your permission, I'd really like to keep this flash drive for a few days so I can examine everything. I think I can give you at least a partial translation of most of these documents."

"That would be great."

"I'm curious, though: How did you know to bring this to me?"

"Why do you ask?" Rachel said, mentally scrambling for an explanation. "You sound like you're the perfect person for this job."

"I might be," Leda replied, a hint of personal pride leaking through her professional smile, "but my background in linguistics isn't advertised on the museum website. How did you know to ask for me when you called?"

Rachel's stomach twisted, but her face remained placid. "A friend recommended you."

"I see . . . May I ask who?"

"Mr. Bach . . . uh, Bridges. Bach Bridges."

"Bridges," Miss Morley mumbled thoughtfully. "I don't remember him." She shrugged. "Well, my boss does parade a lot of people through here. I probably forget half of their names before they even leave the building." She smiled again, easing Rachel's nerves. "Please thank him for me. This is the most fascinating thing I've seen in years. I'm really looking forward to working on it."

"Great!" Rachel stood up and pulled on her coat. "I'll leave you to it. You have my cell number. Let me know when you find something. I can't wait to know what my uncle was up to."

"That makes two of us."

Miss Morley held out her hand and Rachel accepted it. The assistant curator's firm grip raised Rachel's estimation of her.

"I'll be in touch soon," Miss Morley promised.

Rachel was halfway to the door when Miss Morley's computer suddenly let loose a noisy series of beeps and electronic wails. The assistant curator's expression flashed alarm, and she quickly returned to her chair. The blinking light of her monitor bounced off her dark skin and lit up her eyes with a red warning banner. Her fingers flew over the keyboard.

Rachel's muscles tensed. "Is something wrong?" she asked anxiously.

"I'm not sure." Miss Morley's forehead was a maze of crinkles. "The computer's telling me that a file on the USB key infected my system . . . which is weird, because I scanned it for viruses when I loaded it."

Rachel recalled performing her own scan, with the same result: no virus detected. A sense of foreboding nibbled at her gut even as the fear of exposure, a constant worry for any Arcanan in her line of work, suddenly reared up. Fighting to keep it from swelling any more, she asked,

"Is there any damage?"

"Doesn't look like it. Actually, I think the virus, if there was one, went after my email. Looks like it sent a message from my computer, but the address has been deleted already." Miss Morley groaned. "You watch—it'll spam my entire department. Did you have this problem when you loaded it on your computer?"

"No, I didn't," Rachel honestly replied. "I'm so sorry. I never would have given it to you if I'd thought there was a problem."

"It's okay." Miss Morley frowned at the computer screen and shook her head dismissively. "I'll call the IT guy, have him look at it." She glanced up at Rachel and smiled distractedly. "I'll take care of it. I'll give you a call as soon as I know something about your files. Thanks again for bringing them to me."

More discomfort crept into Rachel's spine and tickled its way up her back to the base of her neck. The memory stick had sent an email? Why? To whom? She thought of the near-soulless man and cringed internally. A man living under the perpetual influence of a daemon. A man who was, until recently, in possession of a flash drive full of peculiar languages and a sneaky virus that evaded detection long enough to shoot off an email. Her mind conjured a wealth of possibilities to explain this madness, none of them pleasant.

Swallowing her concern, she forced a smile, nodded at Miss Morley, and quietly slipped out the door. All the way down the hall, she let her eyes drift aimlessly over the long line of office doors, inhaling the dusty scent of book binding and printer ink, as her worries whispered in her ear like the sickly sweet temptations of an unseen daemon.

COINCIDENCE

Bach kept a respectful distance from the slinking brown coat as he watched it creep around the house. Curious though he was, the sight of a coat that moved all on its own dredged up a primitive fear in him that froze his feet to the floor every time he tried to edge his way closer. The only time it passed close to him (it appeared around a corner unexpectedly, causing Bach to jump backward), he snuck a glimpse down the open neck hole. There was nothing inside. The coat was moving as if suspended in midair by a puppeteer's strings. At this revelation, all of Bach's hair stood on end and his heart leapt like a rabbit that's just heard a hawk's hungry shriek. From that moment on, he was ever vigilant, intent on making sure the coat did not catch him unaware. He followed it and watched it and tried not to think too hard about what was making it move.

Rachel arrived home close to five o'clock with her eyes full of thought. Much to Bach's surprise, she walked right past the shuffling coat without so much as a glance, yet she shot a brief glare in his direction. She seemed less concerned with the coat's presence than she was with his.

"You're still here?" she mumbled.

His stomach lurched at her irritated tone. "Well," he said quietly, "I have nowhere else to go."

She looked him up and down. There was a strange mix of intensity and detachment in her face, as if she was a scientist studying a specimen. Bach shifted his weight, uncertain of his place in her home and fearful of returning to the larger world, where the only roof over his head was a rusted bridge. Rachel took off her jacket and tossed it over the banister. Then she brushed past Bach and headed for the kitchen.

"You can't stay here forever," she said over her shoulder. "You're Notan. This is an Arcanan house. You don't belong here."

Bach started after her, but the coat drifted across the kitchen threshold, blocking his path. He stared at it, silently willing it to move, but instead it settled down, its fabric crumpling like a balloon losing half its air. With one hand on the doorframe and his feet firmly planted, Bach leaned as far inside the kitchen as he could without making contact with the thing. From where he was, he couldn't see Rachel, but he could hear her moving around.

"How long will you let me stay?" he called out.

He heard her take a long, deep breath. The refrigerator door opened and then closed. There was a soft clatter as dishes and silverware were moved around. He waited, holding his breath so as not to miss a sound.

"I don't know," she finally groaned. "I don't wanna think about it right now. Are you hungry?"

"Hell yeah."

"I'm making burgers. Want one?"

The mention of food made his mouth water like a busted faucet. With his sanity only recently returned, he couldn't remember when he had eaten last, but he knew his stomach was painfully empty. Fear of the future persisted in his mind, but his famished body demanded that he let it take precedence. "Sounds great. Thanks."

The coat stirred. Hoping it would move just a foot or two so he could squeeze by, Bach started to inch forward, but when the coat turned in a circle and settled back into the same spot, he stopped cold. He accidentally peered down the neck again and quickly whipped his gaze away when confronted with the empty space inside.

His stomach growled insistently. Though he was still disturbed by the coat's presence, the promise of food overran his fear. Very gingerly, he lifted one leg, stepped over the motionless coat, and eased his other leg over. Then he walked backward into the kitchen, eyes locked on the coat. It didn't budge.

"Hey," he said. "What's with the coat?"

"Huh?" Rachel glanced at him and then the threshold, and seemed to notice the old piece of clothing for the first time. "Oh, that. It's a daemon."

His heart skipped a beat. "The coat is a demon?"

Rachel laughed aloud. The purity of the sound surprised him. Somehow, he had startled her into a moment of genuine happiness. For the first time since returning home, she looked him in the eye.

"No." She was still laughing. "The daemon is wearing the coat."

"'Wearing'? But there's nothing inside. I looked."

"You can't see daemons with your naked eye. Well," she qualified, "some people can, but that's not a talent anyone would want. Most of those people are pretty messed up."

"Messed up how?"

"Like you under the bridge," she said, her eyes piercing him with their severity, "but much worse."

It was a sobering thought. Of all the homeless folks who'd made their homes under the bridge, Bach had easily been the craziest of the crazies. The rest of the population, even those suffering from their own delusions, had walked a wide circle around him like he was a bristling porcupine. The idea of someone being in worse shape than that was difficult to grasp.

"You can't see them either, right?" He glanced at the coat and thought of the emptiness it contained. "Then how do you catch them?"

"Here." She handed him a mixing bowl. "Mix up the beef, egg, and all that stuff. I'll be back in just a second."

The rich aroma of meat and herbs filled his nose and set his stomach gurgling. He plunged his hands into the bowl and mashed the ingredients together, listening to the sound of Rachel's retreating footsteps. The beef mixture was bitingly cold—his fingers grew numb within seconds of contact—but his heart warmed as he worked. The feel and the scent stirred memories of assisting his grandmother before Fourth of July cookouts. He smiled at the thought of her and heard her kind voice in his ear as he separated the mix into four patties. Every thought of her brought a muddle of nostalgia, love, and grief, but he never shied away from the memories. They were all he had of her, and he loved every single one.

Once finished with the meat, he immediately turned on the kitchen sink to as hot as the water would get and scrubbed away the frigid pain in his fingers. Even as he washed away the mush on his skin, the scent was so enticing that he was sorely tempted to eat the burgers raw. He looked down at the clothes hanging limply from his wasted body. Before his breakdown, the shirt and jeans would have fit him perfectly, but that was six months and almost forty pounds ago. A shower, shave, and some clean clothes may have returned him to the world of the living, but the road to recovery still stretched into the distance.

Rachel returned as he was drying his hands, a pair of glasses in her hand. His brows furrowed into a question mark.

"Put these on," she said, "and then go look at the coat. Just don't be freaked out."

He accepted the glasses but didn't put them on right away. Instead, he turned them over in his hands, feeling the smooth metal, plastic, and glass with his fingertips. They appeared ordinary except for an eerie glimmer on the lenses, something like the reflection of a rainbow on cloudy ice. He glanced over Rachel's shoulder, to where he had last seen the coat, and narrowed his blue eyes with suspicion. It was gone.

Rachel followed his gaze. "I think it's in the living room," she said.

Before Bach could ask the question stirring behind his lips, she answered it unbidden.

"It won't hurt you. It's defective, but its defect makes it more or less harmless."

Still, he hesitated.

"Go on," she urged. "Go check it out."

Regardless of her assurances, the thought of the vacant yet mobile coat still prickled the animal fear in Bach's chest. When he made no move to leave the kitchen, Rachel rolled her eyes and hooked her hand under his elbow. With a little tugging, he finally walked with her.

She led him to the foyer and then on to the living room. "Daemon! Come over here and stay close to me! Let my guest have a look at you."

The old brown coat appeared from behind an armchair and waddled in her direction, the ends of its sleeves dragging in its wake. Panic exploded in Bach's blood, but Rachel's hand on his elbow anchored him to the spot.

The thing wearing the coat came to a stop at his feet and stood still. Bach turned his head every which way to avoid looking down the center of the garment again; knowing there was an invisible creature there didn't make the empty spot less horrible.

"Put the glasses on," Rachel instructed him, but he could barely hear her over his own racing heartbeat.

Very slowly, and only after several nudges from her, he closed his eyes, unfolded the glasses, and squeezed them onto his face. *A demon*, he thought, his mind racing. *Am I really going to look at a demon?*

Once the glasses were on, he took a deep breath and opened his eyes.

The room was afloat with swirling colors, ghostly blips, and fractals that floated and drifted on air currents he could not feel. A sudden puff of breath from his lips sent the nearest bunch spiraling away, causing him to jerk back in astonishment. The air was so full of outlandish patterns and smudged colors, it seemed thick in a way he could almost taste. He swiped at the closest snowflake-like pattern, and his fingers passed through the thing without resistance. But it also smeared slightly from the contact, like paint under a brush. As Bach watched, it steadily drew itself back together into a similar but not identical shape, even as it moved very slowly in the direction he had swept his hand. Its color fluctuated gradually from crystal green to neon yellow and then, as it intersected with a snakelike wisp of blue, it transformed into a crimson sphere. It was alien but beautiful, fragile but enduring. It filled his eyes and occupied all his thought.

It was suffocating.

Bach's legs began to shake and his breath grew choppy. Behind the glasses, his blue eyes grew wide and began to twitch. Inside his head, the newly restored order that was keeping his sight-beyond from cluttering his mind was rapidly breaking down. The information his strange gift made available to him was shaking loose from the recesses where it was housed, interrupting his regular thought process. He became light-headed and swayed.

Rachel grabbed his arm and lunged for the glasses, but not in time. Bach collapsed to the floor, landing on the area rug with a thud that spewed a cloud of dust into the living room air.

In the last seconds before losing consciousness, he caught a glimpse of the coat through the lenses. From within its folds, a long, pointed, green ear stuck out at an angle and one big, bulging eye with no iris stared at him with naked disinterest.

BACH AWOKE WITH a dull headache and a pain in his shoulder from where he had struck the floor. He opened his eyes to a blaze of lamplight that stung him like a slap to the face. The glasses were gone; the bizarre fractals and crystalline shapes were nowhere to be seen. Order was quickly being restored to his mind. Still, he didn't seem to have recovered his balance yet; the floor seemed to slant one way or another as he tried to move.

The adrenaline gradually drained out of his muscles, but his body still shook from its presence. When he pushed himself up, trembling, Rachel grabbed his shoulder and held him still.

"Stay where you are," she said. "You've been seizing again. Are you okay?"

"Yeah," he muttered. "What the hell happened?"

"I screwed up," she said, an unspoken apology on her face. "They told me during my training that oracles are unfit to be daemon collectors, but I never understood why. I guess I know now. Makes sense." She helped him rise slowly to his feet. "An oracle's brain is wired differently than the average person's."

Though he heard her words, they sounded a little strange to his recovering ears, almost as if she had slipped into another language. Struggling to comprehend what she was saying, he pressed one hand to his face, breathed deep, and tried to focus.

"What?"

"You see the world in a different way," she explained. "Your senses are tuned to a slightly different frequency and your brain stores information differently."

As the effects of the seizure faded and reality became crisper, Bach was able to wrap his mind around her words and grasp their meaning.

"So . . . I couldn't use the glasses . . . because I'm different."

"Yes. You shouldn't use anything that alters your perception. You'll wind up frying your mind."

"My 'different' mind."

"Right." She smiled meekly, loose strands of her dark brown hair falling across her small face, and shrugged. "My fault. I'm sorry."

Her eyes reflected the truth of her words, and Bach took them to heart. It was just an accident. Balance returned to him and he straightened up. His shoulder still hurt a bit, but his headache was already gone. Realizing that he had just seen something most people would never even know existed, he decided the lingering pain was worth it.

"It's all right. I'm kinda glad I got to see the demon." He glanced around as they made their way back through the house to the kitchen. He didn't see the coat. "Where is it?"

"Wandered away. It does that."

"Yeah." A thought occurred and Bach fixed Rachel in a worried squint. "He's not gonna watch me while I sleep or anything, is he?"

"'It,'" she corrected, "not 'he.' And no, it won't."

"The demon's not a he?"

"Ninety-nine percent of daemons are sexless, and the ones that have a sex . . ." She raised one eyebrow. "Well, let's just say it's very obvious. Anyway, that's a riot daemon. All riot daemons are sexless."

Bach took a seat at the kitchen table and let the last little tears in his sanity knit themselves back together while Rachel fired up the stovetop and got the burgers cooking. He enjoyed the faint flow of heat through the coolness of the house, as well as the delightful smell of the cooking meat.

"You pronounce the word *demon* strangely," he said. "Is that a second-language slipup?"

"No," she said through the smoke rising from the pan. "They're two different words. A daemon—there's an *a* before the *e*—is a type of creature that tempts human beings to act in a particular way via subconscious whispers. All types of daemons break down now and then."

"Who put you guys in charge of the demons—sorry, daemons?" he asked. "Was it God?"

"You think I'm a divine messenger?" she scoffed. She

glanced up from the burgers with a flat expression. "You're not much of an oracle if you do."

"But how do your people even know about daemons?" he pressed. "Who discovered them?"

"I don't know who discovered them," she said. "Knowledge of daemons actually came to us from another, older dimension."

"Older . . ." Bach's eyes widened like a gaping mouth, striving to swallow this information. "How old?"

"Um . . ." Rachel checked the underside of one meat patty. "Very old. See, the Arcana has been around since before recorded Notan history. Our current social structure, including daemon monitoring, was established tens of thousands of years ago when some refugees from an older, decaying human dimension joined our world. Using the knowledge we gained from them, daemon monitoring became part of the fabric of our society. It's . . . it's just the way things are."

Just the way things are. Like an adult casually justifying table manners to a child.

"You've spent your whole life keeping this world—the, uh . . . the Nota world—running smoothly just because 'it's the way things are'?" He shook his head, dumbfounded. "That's all?"

"That's the life I was born into," she replied simply.

"So you're cool with it?"

"Yes."

He shook his head again and ran his hands through his hair. Daemons, different dimensions, glasses that showed the wearer outrageous wonders—it boggled his mind that she was so numb to it all.

"I think that's weird."

She flipped the burgers. The meat sizzled. "I think it's weird that you think it's weird."

"Seriously?"

"Yes," she snapped, startling him. "Know what else I think is weird? I think it's weird that you live your whole life as a citizen of a country that goes to war with other countries despite the fact that you all share the same world. I think it's weird that you pay people to govern you. I think it's weird that you let a handful of people live in obscene excess while thousands of others starve. I think it's weird that you deny education and medical treatment to people based solely on their inability to pay for it. I think it's weird that you use energy sources that you know are making your water undrinkable and your air unbreathable. I think it's weird that you accumulate so much garbage that you have to have it hauled away on a weekly basis so it can rot in a landfill. And you know what I really think is weird, Bach?" She pointed the spatula at him, jabbing for emphasis. "Manicured lawns. You people pay money for a home with land around it, and then you use the land to grow nothing but grass, which you then cut short as soon as it grows. What is the point of having land if you're not going to grow something useful on it? At the very least, let the grass grow and get some sheep to trim it for you. Sheep have a dozen uses! Grass, not so much." She wrinkled her nose as if the meat had suddenly started to stink. "You people make no fucking sense."

Bach stared at her in stunned silence and tried to absorb the impact of the culture clash that had just slammed into him. Since meeting her, he had known at least superficially that Rachel was from a faraway place; but she looked and sounded and acted like any other person he might meet, so up until this point he had not given her origins much thought. As he looked at her now, in the wake of her outburst, he saw something different. The clothes she wore (jeans and a long-sleeve top) looked conventional enough, but, upon closer inspection, they lacked distinctive logos and tags. She wore no obvious makeup, and, unlike most women he knew, she made no effort to keep her fingernails manicured. She wore no jewelry other than a wristwatch, and her earlobes were unpierced. She looked and sounded and acted like the average person, but that, he now realized, was because she had been trained to do those things; she had been taught, extensively, not to stand out. The place she came from must not be at all like the world he had grown up in. *My God*, he suddenly thought. *How homesick she must be.*

"Sorry," he said quietly. "I didn't mean to offend you."

"No big deal," she mumbled.

She placed two plates near the stove top and arranged the buns on top of them before putting two burgers on each plate. After adding lettuce and cheese, she brought the plates to the table, set them down, and shoved one under his nose.

"Enjoy," she said.

The swirling aromas of hot beef and melting cheese filled his nostrils and set his mouth to watering. His empty stomach roared with anticipation. He grabbed the nearest burger with both hands and tore into it.

The first bite filled his mouth with flavors so rich and juices so savory they brought tears to his eyes. He set his elbows on the tabletop, lowered his head, and heaved a sigh through his nose as one escaped tear rolled down his cheek. With a sharp sniff, he quickly swiped it away, sat up, and inhaled the rest of the burger. He grabbed the second one without pausing to breathe. He had eaten nothing half so good in the last six months. Even as he felt his shrunken belly fill to capacity, he didn't want to stop.

"This is delicious," he said, his mouth full. "Thank you."

"You're welcome."

The second burger half eaten and his hunger appeased, his attention drifted from the remaining food to Rachel. Still on her first burger, she took small bites and chewed slowly, her eyes trained on the window. The taste of the food, a constant delight to him, seemed not to interest her; the mechanical way she consumed the burger suggested to him that she saw it only as fuel, not as an experience. It saddened him to think that she wasn't enjoying the meal as deeply as he was. She had created something marvelous but didn't appreciate it. That was a shame.

Her eyes lit upon something in the backyard, and her face tightened slightly. "I don't remember a tree there," she mumbled under her breath.

Bach looked and saw a spindly sapling, little more than a leafless twig, emerging from the lawn. It looked lonesome in that bare yard, the tallest plant in a lake of waving grass, but it also looked determined. Despite its isolation, it was managing to grow. He thought he should find it inspiring, but somehow, he couldn't shake the feeling that it was out of place and should be removed.

Rachel didn't look like she shared his distrust. She just looked glazed. "The plants around this house grow so fast," she mused, still chewing. "I wonder if it's part of how this pocket dimension functions."

To be reminded that he was sitting in a house-sized ball of reality made Bach shift his weight in his seat. He couldn't stop picturing the house and its surroundings as a toy top, spinning wildly on a jet-black marble slab. The image made him shiver.

Rachel's eyes were glossy and distant as she stared at the

tree. Now eager for something to break the silence, Bach sniffed loudly.

"So . . . did you meet with Leda Morley?"

"Yeah." The look of deep thought that he had noticed when Rachel first came home returned to her sharp brown eyes as she said, "She's happy to work on it."

Her voice sounded uncommitted, unconvinced.

Sensing there was more at play, he asked, "Is there a problem?"

"Well . . . something strange happened."

In between bites, Rachel recounted the story of the apparent computer virus that had fired off an email from Miss Morley's account. Bach listened attentively while shoveling the last few bites of his food in his mouth. As she wrapped up, he leaned back in his chair, rested his hands on his bulging stomach, and turned the events over in his mind.

"Did it do the same thing to your laptop?" he asked.

"No," she said, the second half of her first burger still in her hand. "I keep trying to tell myself that it must have been a glitch in her computer, but it just seems like too big a coincidence." She took another bite and chewed it slowly, her eyes drifting to the window again. "You're an oracle," she finally said. "You learn about things before they happen all the time. To you, life must seem like a . . . rerun."

"Sometimes," he agreed. "My sight-beyond does make it harder to be surprised."

She cocked her head at him. "So do you believe in coincidences?"

"Yeah," he said confidently. "They happen every day."

Rachel took another bite, looked down at her plate, and then pushed it toward Bach, who eagerly accepted. As he took two huge bites of his third burger of the evening in quick succession, she leaned her chin on her knuckles and looked at him thoughtfully.

"Do you believe meeting me was a coincidence?"

"No way," he said, his mouth stuffed full. "This definitely happened for a reason. No way could it be a coincidence that I crossed your path and you just happened to be the person who could not only snap me out of the crazies but could also put a name to my extra sense. Not a coincidence. Nuh-uh." He swallowed and looked her in the eye. "I guess you could say that I believe coincidences happen but, knowing the things I know, I tend to look at them with a little suspicion."

"Right," she said. "So how would you look at the memory stick and the virus? Coincidence?"

"He was—hold up!" A rush of stimuli flooded Bach's brain like a dam had just broken. He put down what little was left of his third burger and stared at the tabletop as the initial wave receded and left a silt of new information in its wake. His eyes vibrated slightly. "I know something. Something about the guy you're looking for."

Rachel straightened up and her eyes zeroed in on him. Her sudden interest was not lost on Bach. Knowing that he had useful information somewhere in his brain, he shoved all other thoughts aside and waited for the bits he wanted, the ones he knew were there somewhere, to surface. That didn't always work, but this time the pieces he was looking for jumped to his conscious mind almost immediately.

"The drive's not his," he announced. "I mean, you got it from him, but he's not the one who put all those files on there. *But.* He did put something on that memory stick to alert him if someone else tried to access the files—fixed it so if someone other than him opened the files, it would send him an email so he'd know where it is, like a . . . homing signal."

Rachel squinted, doubtful. "But nothing happened when I opened the files on my laptop."

"I know. That is a puzzler. But your laptop's from the Arcana, right? Maybe your system is too different from his for the homing signal to activate. Or maybe it has something to do with this house being in a pocket dimension. Maybe the signal didn't activate because your laptop isn't in the same world. I don't know. I don't know shit about computers. Doesn't matter anyway. What matters is that he knows Leda Morley has his flash drive, and he wants it back." Urgency crept into his voice as a sense of dread washed over him. "He wants it back, like, *now*."

The alarm in his tone spread to Rachel like a virus; she sat up straight with her hands balled tight, ready to throw a punch. "Fuck!" she shrieked, hammering both fists on the table, and then jumped up so abruptly that her chair toppled to the floor. "I *knew* something was wrong! I *knew* it! I shouldn't have left that thing with her!" She flew out of the kitchen.

Bach jumped up from his seat, his burger still in his hand. "Where're you going?"

"Back to the museum," she shouted as she threw on her coat. "I gotta catch that guy before he gets to her!"

Bach's sight-beyond wailed, alarming him. Heart thundering, he hurried after her. "Should I go with you?"

"You'd be in the way!"

The accusation stung, but he realized that she was right. He knew nothing about her job and next to nothing about her target, and his wasted body was a pale imitation of its former self. In his current state, he wouldn't be much use to anyone. Disrupting Rachel's work was no way to repay his debt to her.

Unhappily resigned, he stood back, well clear of her path, as she charged out of the house, not bothering to close the door behind her. His sight-beyond continued to blare its distress as he watched her run up the front path into the darkness, where she was swallowed up without a trace.

Bach stood in the doorway and stared at the spot where Rachel had disappeared, her final words to him echoing in his ears. He looked down at himself. The shower and shave had given him his face back, but his body was another matter: he had very little muscle definition and virtually no body fat; his arms were spindly, his legs were unsteady, and his chest was far narrower than it had been since before he hit puberty. Shoving aside his residual sight-beyond distress, he sighed a tired, depressed sigh. He would have to find another way to help—one that didn't require physical strength.

The coat shuffled close to him, headed to the front door. Bach glanced down at it and was pleased to discover that he was no longer afraid. True, there was a demon—no, a daemon—under that coat, but its presence no longer unnerved him. Having seen it, he'd decided that it wasn't any more menacing than an ugly garden gnome. Unlike all the people he'd met throughout his life, he received no images, facts, or impressions from the daemon, except for the feeling that the creature couldn't care less that he existed. That suited him fine. It was better, in his opinion, to be uninteresting to inhuman things; he couldn't imagine that being interesting to a daemon was a safe or healthy way to live.

As the daemon passed close to him, Bach held out the last bit of his dinner in its direction.

"Hungry?" he asked politely.

The coat stopped and its posture shifted, as if the thing

inside it was looking up at him. It stood there only a few seconds before resuming its course and crossing over the threshold. From there, it bounced down the front steps and waddled up the path toward the passage.

Bach stepped out onto the porch and watched as it followed in Rachel's footsteps and faded into darkness. Briefly, he wondered where it was going and whether he should have tried to stop it, but he quickly decided that it was not his business to direct a daemon. It was soon out of sight and, for Bach, out of mind.

He looked at the smooshed remains of the burger in his hand. The bun was compressed, the cheese was all but gone, and the lettuce was nothing but a smear of green. He was sure it would still be the most delicious bit of mush he'd ever eaten, but he was full. He was beyond full. He hadn't eaten half this much at one meal for so long that his stomach had become nothing but a sliver of an organ. Now it was stretched and distended so badly that his torso actually ached. Still, he couldn't bear to waste such excellent food. He stared at it longingly, painfully.

"What to do?" he whispered.

From under his feet, he heard a soft whine. Startled, he immediately dropped to his knees and peered through a crack in the porch floor. Seeing a flicker of movement, a little dart of a shadow, he stood, descended the steps, and looked through the broken cross-hatching. There was precious little light, but after a moment his eyes adjusted sufficiently to see the animal hidden beneath the house.

It was a puppy. Its fur was covered in mud, but Bach smiled like an enchanted child at the sight of it. He knelt in the dirt and reached his hand through the broken slats.

"Hi, pup," he said. "What're you doing under there, huh?" He held out the remnants of the burger, offering it to the dog on a flat palm. "Are you hungry?"

The dog whined again. Slowly, haltingly, it started crawling toward him while licking its chops and wagging its tail. It creeped toward the burger, but its eyes stayed fixed on Bach in a silent plea for mercy and kindness. The young man's heart warmed and overflowed at the sight of another living being looking to him for comfort.

As the puppy gulped down the morsel and then returned to lick the juice from his fingers, Bach felt his wasted body flush with energy. Very gently, he stretched a few more inches through the cross-hatching and patted the dog on the back of its neck. The animal stiffened at first and flashed its teeth, its fur standing on end, but its snarl quickly melted into a sigh and it leaned into the caress.

Bach beamed from ear to ear as the puppy tilted over and rolled onto its back, its tender belly exposed for a rub, its tongue lolling through a canine smile, and its eyes wide with instant love.

11
STAKEOUT

The Rigaceen Museum was closed for the night, but a few lights still burned for the benefit of the last employees on the premises. As she approached the building, Rachel recalled her earlier visit and used what she remembered to estimate where Miss Morley's office might be. Based on her memory of left and right turns in the hallways and the view she had seen through the window, her best guess brought her to the back of the museum. It took half an hour of loitering in the cold evening air before she finally spotted Miss Morley in one of the lighted offices. She breathed a sigh of relief, not only to have found the right office but also to see that Miss Morley was safe. The owner of the flash drive had clearly not found her—yet.

Rachel picked a spot that she felt would be difficult to see from inside the museum and settled in. Her target was sure to show up eventually, and when he did, she would be waiting.

The curator's assistant looked to be hard at work, striding in and out of the room like a woman on a mission with her arms full of books, boxes, and folders of various sizes. She walked with her shoulders back and her head held high and wore an expression of calm determination. Her bearing impressed

Rachel. Living in the Nota for an extended period sometimes left her disheartened and frustrated—largely because of how women were treated and expected to behave, and what that did to their morale. But seeing someone like Miss Morley, who displayed an almost Arcanan level of confidence, made her feel that this dimension wasn't so far behind her own.

She saw Miss Morley's pride falter, however, when a chubby bald man in a gray suit walked into her office without knocking and pushed some papers aside so he could perch one butt cheek on the edge of her desk, despite the empty chair right in front of him. At this, the glow of the young woman's face dimmed and darkened. She looked the man in the eye and held a neutral expression, but her head lowered visibly as he talked at her.

"He's a jackass, isn't he?" Rachel said, her breath now visible in the cold. "If you had a choice, you'd push him off your desk and kick his ass out the door. He's probably your boss. I can't imagine you'd put up with him if he wasn't."

The bald man continued talking for several minutes, during which time Miss Morley nodded occasionally but never said a word. At last, he stood up (knocking over a picture frame on her desk in the process, a move he made no attempt to correct), stuck his meaty hands in his pockets, and strolled out the door. As soon as he was out of sight, Miss Morley's lip curled like a snarling dog's and she rolled her eyes. Rachel smirked and nodded approvingly.

Evening wore into night. One by one, the lights blinked out all over the building, and yet Miss Morley's office still gleamed bright. Rachel found an old crate to sit on and tried in vain to make herself comfortable without compromising her focus. With every hour that passed, there were fewer and fewer people present who might get between her mark and the woman who had his property. Very soon, there would be no witnesses. The later Miss Morley worked, the more she played into the hands of the nearly soulless man.

Though she was desperate to catch her mark, Rachel was growing increasingly uncomfortable with using a young woman as bait. She knew what the man was capable of; he was not bothered by violence and, thanks to the daemon attached to him, he was single-minded in his pursuit of his goals. Miss Morley might as well be a wounded seal dangling over a shark tank.

She toyed with the idea of bursting into the woman's office and telling her she was in danger, but years of training had hammered into her the necessity of a low profile. She had already brought one Notan into her business that day; she wasn't about to bring another. No, this was her best chance to catch the guy. If Miss Morley had to be bait to accomplish that, then so be it. Squashing her conscience, she hugged herself against the night's chill and waited.

It was just past eight o'clock when Rachel felt a soft tug on the end of her jeans. She glanced down and, to her great surprise, saw a familiar brown coat pressed against the side of her makeshift seat. A moment of stunned denial quickly gave way to anger.

"What the fuck?"

"Catch," said the daemon.

"What are you doing here?" she snapped. "You're supposed to be at the house."

The coat trembled and released its hold on her jeans. "'Stay close me.'"

If Rachel could have shot lightning from her eyes, she

would have. She could hardly believe the insanity of hearing her own words quoted by a daemon.

"I didn't mean you should stay close to me all night," she hissed through her teeth. "I'm on the job, you pest!"

The daemon retreated into the depths of the old coat.

"Catch say," it protested. "Catch say."

"Unbelievable!" she said. "You've been around humans for your entire existence. Are you trying to tell me that with all that exposure, you can't wrap your tiny, daemonic mind around the basic meanings of human speech?"

"Catch say," repeated the peculiar, echoing voice. "Catch say."

"I—oh, forget it," she said. "I can't deal with you now. Either go home and be sure no one sees you on the way or stay close—not too close—and wait for me. Either way, shut up and don't touch me."

The coat obediently slunk away and hunkered down behind the crate, taking great care not to touch her as it moved. Rachel followed it with her eyes and glared until she was confident that it was going to stay still. Only then did she return her gaze to the window above.

The moment she did, she jolted. The face from the picture in her assignment file, the face attached to the elbow that had struck her in the head, was standing in Miss Morley's doorway.

"That's him!" she blurted. "That's my mark!"

He was speaking now, his prematurely aged face grim with determination. Her heart in her throat, Rachel leapt to her feet and stood with her feet planted and her fists balled at her sides. She couldn't hear what he was saying, but from the way he was pointing emphatically at Miss Morley, she guessed that he was demanding his flash drive.

Miss Morley, meanwhile, was standing, her purse slung over her shoulder, as if she had been about to leave when her uninvited visitor stopped her. She leaned forward, her shoulders squared and her hands planted firmly on the desk that separated her from the intruder. Then, with a grand gesture worthy of an imperial viceroy, she swept her arm in a wide arc, pointed at the door, and shouted a command while staring the man directly in the eye.

The man's nostrils flared and his lip curled. With the speed of a striking viper, he lunged across Miss Morley's desk and grabbed for her arm.

Rachel felt a bolt of adrenaline shoot through her veins. Not waiting for the inevitable struggle to begin, she sprang from her hiding place and sprinted for the nearest door.

Breaching locked buildings was an area of training in which Rachel had excelled, and the lock on the back door of the museum was both antiquated and poorly fitted; it fell to pieces in seconds and the door swung open without a sound. Panting, Rachel sprinted through the building, trying to mentally hold the location of Miss Morley's office as the focal point of her movement. She navigated the twists and turns of the hallways frantically but deliberately, and after what seemed like ages, she came to the hallway she had walked just hours earlier and spotted the light from Miss Morley's room spilling through the open door. She dashed to the young woman's office and stopped dead on the threshold. The room was empty.

A shout came from around the hallway corner, a frightened but vicious cry. Rachel's head snapped toward the sound. Leda Morley's tone had shifted dramatically, from the polite and proper voice of a career woman to the spitfire tenor of a girl who was prepared to fight for her life.

"Get your hands off me!" she screamed. "Help!"

Rachel took only two steps in the direction of the shouting before a loud clap—the crack of skin on skin—silenced Leda. The sudden quiet engulfed Rachel and amplified every little step and creak of her joints. Rachel caught her breath and froze with her left foot several inches off the ground. Her well-toned muscles held the position with minimum strain, but her fear-struck heart forced blood through her veins too fast for her liking. She slowly, gently put one hand on the nearby wall and carefully lowered her foot to the ground while straining her ears over her thundering heart to hear around the corner for any hint of a coming attack. All she heard was a muffled groan, probably Miss Morley, and then a shuffling sound.

Rachel listened as intently as her roaring heartbeat would allow and tried to identify the scrapes and thumps she was hearing.

He's going through her pockets, she finally realized. *She's unconscious and he's rolling her over to reach all her pockets. He's looking for the memory stick.*

The shuffling sound gave way to a muffled clatter, the sound of him riffling through her purse, as Rachel tried to inch her way closer to the corner. Her steps were small and painfully slow. Deep in her mind, the scratchy voice of an old instructor scolded her for every potential misstep she was making. She could picture him as he was years ago, gray and bent and heavily scarred, his one razor of an eye slicing into every student who crossed his path. *"Being a collector,"* she heard him telling her, *"is to be one-part hunter, one-part con artist, and one-part burglar. If you can't be all three, you're not a whole collector."*

Rachel kept his voice in her head with every step she took, with every motion of her arms, with every touch of her fingers. The corner was within reach when she came to a gradual stop and listened closely again.

The noise had stopped, and in its place was a stark silence so thick it was like syrup in her ears. She held her breath and tilted her head. No sound at all. Then a chuckle exploded in the air, shattering the hush. She bit back a gasp.

"Pretty," said the man. She recognized the voice. It was the same voice that had called her a bitch earlier that day. "Damn shame to bust up her cheek like that."

There was a soft drumming sound. Rachel guessed he was tapping his fingers on something. He sighed and clucked his tongue while shifting his weight from one foot to the other.

What's he doing? Rachel wondered. *If he's got what he came for, why isn't he leaving?*

The man chuckled again. "What the hell," he said pleasantly. "I'm done with the last one anyway."

Rachel's brow furrowed and her face tightened in confusion. *Last one? Done with? What does that mean?*

Her musing was cut short by a muted tussling, accompanied by another groan from Miss Morley. The man grunted a little and exhaled with a growl, and then his footsteps, conspicuously heavier than before, moved down the hallway, away from Rachel. Slowly, she slid to the corner and peered around the edge. She caught a glimpse of the man's back as he opened the door to the stairwell. Her stomach dropped and every hair on her skin crackled with horror and alarm.

"Shit," she whispered.

Leda Morley's limp body was slung over his shoulder. The heavy door swung shut behind him with a metallic thud.

BASEMENT DOOR

"**Y**ou're *where?*"

"I'm following my human mark," Rachel panted. "He's in a car."

"And you're on foot?"

"Where else would I be?" she snapped. "I can't wait on a bus and I can't drive a car any more than you can!"

She continued running with the cell phone clutched in her hand. Houses, bus stops, civilians, and yappy dogs on leashes blinked in and out of her vision as she raced along the avenue. People occasionally made little exclamations of surprise or indignation as she blew past them, but she knew she would be out of their thoughts within seconds of passing. That was the peculiar loneliness of this world: a distressed young woman running down the street as fast as she could go attracted only enough attention to annoy those in her path; no one thought to be alarmed or to check on her to be sure that she was okay. She was an oddity but also, as far as these people were concerned, no one's business but her own. Willing isolation seemed to Rachel like a horrible way to live, but this cognitive dissonance made operating in the Nota simpler (it was easier to stay out of sight when no one wanted to see), and tonight, she was grateful for everyone's inattention. If some well-meaning person tried to slow her down, she might lose sight of the gray sedan rolling its way through traffic.

"What street?" asked the voice in her phone.

"Fifth."

"Heading which way?"

"East."

"And you're still on his tail?"

"The lights are against him," she panted. "He keeps hitting reds."

"And he's got a hostage? Who?"

"Is that really important, Suarez? He's got a hostage. End of discussion."

There was a short pause filled only by the patter of Rachel's racing feet and the jagged sound of her breathing.

The voice on the other end of the call mumbled something, half chuckling, in a humorless tone and said, "Eventually you're going to tell me what kind of rules you've broken, right?"

"Later," she promised. "If I tell you now, you'll be on the hook for it. If you don't know, you won't be in trouble."

"Appreciate it," he said. "Could you call the Notan police? This sounds like something more in their line of interest than ours."

"Would *you* like to explain to the Central Office how my mark ended up in Notan custody?"

There was a beat of silence on the other end of the line that lasted just long enough for Rachel to picture Suarez tightening his square jaw and shaking his head.

"No," he admitted. "Okay. What is it you need from me? Backup?"

"For starters. I also need a line to the office. Have you gotten through lately?"

"No and that's really bizarre." There was an edge to Suarez's voice, a seasoning of frustration and anger she'd heard from him before when things were not as he would have them be. "I talked to Benny just before you called, and he can't reach them either. It's like the whole system has gone down. That's never happened before."

"I need their help!" she shouted. "If the office is locked down, where am I supposed to take this guy if I get him? If I actually catch up to him and he doesn't kill me, there's no way I can hold him for long!"

"Okay." Suarez sighed and hissed through his teeth, something he did when he was pulling his thoughts together. Hearing it stirred mixed emotions in Rachel. On the one hand, it meant the situation was serious. On the other hand, when Suarez put his focus into a problem, no situation was hopeless.

"Okay," he repeated. "I'll call Benny, get him to hound the office until they respond. I'll tell him to kick down the door if he has to. I'll call Wu and the both of us will get on your heels. When your guy gets where he's going, send me the address and I'll pass it along. I'm on this, Wilde," he assured her, his voice steady and confident. "I'm on it from this end, so you just concentrate on following him and getting us an address."

"Right." Despite her desperation, his words calmed her a bit. Suarez often had that effect. "How long until you reach me?"

"I'm leaving right now. I should get to you in . . . about an hour."

"An hour?" she shouted frantically. "An hour?"

"The office is closed, Wilde," he reminded her. "That means the cross-city passages are down. I gotta take the long way round. If we're lucky, Wu will be closer, but an hour's the best I can do."

"Shit! Okay, just hurry."

"I'm already moving."

An hour. Miss Morley would be a prisoner for an hour. *And it's my fault.* If she wasn't so busy running, Rachel was sure she would puke.

AFTER LEAVING THE Rigaceen Museum, Rachel had followed the kidnapper at a distance, keeping out of his sight but maintaining him in hers, until they reached the dimly lit parking lot.

Aside from a scattering of cars, it was deserted. Rachel watched her mark drop Miss Morley's limp body into the trunk of his car—no, she realized, not just inside the trunk but inside a footlocker in the trunk. The man closed one lid and then the other, double-locking the curator's assistant inside.

Rachel watched all this happen from behind an empty minivan, all the time trying not to feel the acidic knot in her stomach as she wondered what this near-soulless criminal had meant by "the last one." She didn't dare attack him now, not while he had Miss Morley under his control. Getting her ass kicked yet again would not help the unconscious hostage escape.

The man got into his car, humming cheerily, and drove away at a leisurely pace. *You would think he does this every day,* Rachel thought. *There's a woman in your trunk! Show a little hustle!* The absurdity of her thought dawned on her twice: the first time immediately after thinking it and the second when she began her foot pursuit of his unhurried vehicle.

Thanks to her mark's casual driving, Rachel was able to keep up as the gray sedan rolled up and down the city streets en route to its destination. It made several turns (always accompanied by the appropriate turn signal) before arriving at a small brick house and pulling into the driveway.

The house was one in a long row of single-family homes, all of them perched like square gargoyles above the narrow street on a short but steep hill. To access the front door, one had to climb a sharp flight of stairs that connected the sidewalk to the covered porch. The driveway, however, had been carved out of the hill like a square cave. After turning into it, the kidnapper's car was swallowed up by the hillside until it was all but invisible to passersby—particularly those who, like most Notans, tried to avoid direct eye contact with strangers whenever possible.

Rachel arrived just in time to see him unload his prisoner. He popped his trunk, lugged the footlocker over the edge, and let it thud to the ground with absolute confidence that his actions were either unnoticed or would be quickly forgotten—which, had Rachel not been there, would have been a perfectly reasonable expectation.

She was so out of breath that she was flirting with a blackout, but she had marked her surroundings well and was able to confidently forward the address to Suarez. Her exhausted lungs burned like an oil fire and her overworked legs were shaking like mad, but she didn't dare obey her body's command to rest. Because of her, there was a woman in a psycho's footlocker who needed help. She scanned the house, still panting, and immediately saw that only two lights were on in the entire building: the front porch light and the tiny light by the basement door, an arm's reach from the parked car. Even as she noticed the basement door, her mark began to drag the footlocker in its direction.

Of course he's taking her in through there, she thought. *Solid brick house built on a slope, basement half-buried in the hill, no sign of any windows—probably not much sound getting out through those walls. He can keep her down there as long as he wants, and no one will be the wiser.*

The cell phone in her hand buzzed, and she pressed her thumb to the screen to activate it. She saw a message from Suarez: *Sit tight. I'll be there in 30–40 minutes, Wu in 20. Do NOT rush in there. DO NOT.*

If she hadn't been out of breath, she would have laughed. Of the four of them (Suarez, Wu, Benny, and herself), she had always been the impulsive one, and the others never let her forget it. Wu had been tickled to fits when, during their English training, he had learned what the word *wild* meant. "Wilde is wild!" he'd cried out, laughing.

Though she was still something of a hothead, Rachel wasn't nearly as brash as she once had been; repetitive training and years of active service had reined in her impulses. But the boys of her square—the group she had trained with— had long memories. They had all known each other at their greenest, and though the in-between years had been long ones, those early impressions had carried through. She would always be the impulsive one, just as Wu would always be the joker, Benny would always be the dreamer, and Suarez would always be the unofficial leader. Some things would never change.

Right now was no exception.

Sorry, Suarez, she thought. *Can't sit tight on this one. In twenty minutes, that woman could be dead, and it'll be my fault. I can't live with that.*

Still panting like a dog locked in a car, she trotted across the street and up the man's driveway, taking great care to stay in the shadows. The basement door had no window, and, as she suspected, no sound leaked from the inside. A quick glance at the three industrial-strength deadbolts securing it in place told her this was not the smartest point of entry.

The front door was illuminated by a porch light (too visible for her liking), but there might be a back door or a window she could try. Anyway, if he was in the basement with Miss Morley, it might be better to enter from the upper levels so he would be less likely to hear her. Maybe she would find him otherwise occupied long enough to grab Miss Morley and run without confronting him. *Yeah*, she thought bitterly, *and maybe raccoons will tap dance out of my butt.*

She hugged her chest and forced her breathing and heart to slow. She wasn't going to luck her way into a quick escape. Odds were she was going to have to fight, and odds were she was going to take a beating. But she had been taught to fight and taught to take a beating without suffering lethal damage, whereas Miss Morley had had no such training. Better that she keep the guy busy than let him spend this time alone with his victim. All she had to do was stay alive and keep him occupied long enough for her backup to arrive.

Rachel steeled herself, holding the image of her home and family in her mind, and moved to the back of the house. She could do this. She would do this.

The back door was closed with a common deadbolt, the kind that Rachel had jimmied hundreds of times. She reached into her pocket for her favorite burglary tool, the lockpick her father had given to her as a birthday present two years earlier. As her fingers closed around it, she moved her other hand to drop her cell phone into the opposite pocket. But before she completed the motion, she heard a loud and peculiar crack. At the same moment, she felt a jolt, almost as if the ground under her feet had jerked, and her head bounced forward with great force.

Rachel grabbed the doorframe and righted herself, but she knew at once that something was not right. While wondering where the sound had come from, she also began to wonder why her eyes weren't focusing. Her mind felt like it was swimming against the current, disconnected from her body. She clutched at the tool in her pocket and dropped her cell phone. Instead of dropping into her pocket, it slid down the side of her coat and fell to the ground with a clank.

Rachel swayed, bewildered, trying to pull herself together. She started to reach for the phone, and that's when her lingering equilibrium snapped like an overtaxed elastic band. She toppled face-first onto the back steps. As her vision went incurably fuzzy, she continued to wonder vaguely and pointlessly what was wrong. At the last moment, she saw a pair of men's shoes just inches from her face. Then her weary eyes closed and her confused mind slipped into oblivion.

HE KNELT OVER the girl with the wood plank he had used to hit her still clutched in his hand. His hard eyes, capped by thick gray brows, took in every inch of her body, as if he was cataloging her various parts. He picked up her cell phone and tried unsuccessfully to turn it on. When the screen remained dark, he decided it had broken when she dropped it and flung the thing over the fence into his neighbor's open trash can.

Lips drawn into a thin line, he knelt down and looked closely at the girl he had knocked out. A memory stirred. He didn't remember her face too clearly, but the color and cut of her coat, as well as the bandages on her hands, gave her away —this was the girl who had attacked him earlier.

"Dumb bitch," he said, shaking his head incredulously. "What do you want with me? You a cop or something?"

That didn't seem likely; tackling people in the street and picking locks was a little gung ho for the typical officer. Still, if she was a cop, he had to find out quickly. He had managed to keep his activities off the public radar thus far. One cop on his doorstep was sure to bring more, and that meant questions and warrants and opening doors that he would prefer remained closed. If she was a cop, he had to get rid of her before the other pigs came snorting around.

He unlocked his back door, grabbed her by one ankle, and dragged her over the threshold.

Once inside, he turned out her pockets. He found a metal lock-picking tool, a credit card bearing the name "Rachel Wilde," and a pair of glasses, but no badge. Still not convinced, he pulled up her shirt and cupped his hands around her breasts, checking for a wire in her bra. Nothing. Probably wasn't a cop. He felt some satisfaction at knowing his activities were still undetected. He was still free to do anything he pleased.

He leaned over her and peered into her unconscious face. Rachel Wilde. He didn't know the name, and nothing in her pockets offered him any clue as to her motivation for following him. Well, he would have to ask her when she woke up, and if she wouldn't volunteer the information, he would have to coax it out of her. He grinned. That wouldn't be a problem.

The women he brought here couldn't talk enough once he got started on them. They offered him any piece of information they might know—location of jewelry, bank account numbers, hidden stashes of cash—once they realized why they were here. They all talked . . . until he shut them up.

The girl on the floor groaned but didn't stir. He took her chin in his hand and turned her head back and forth, evaluating her. Small, tanned, athletic—unappealing. She looked a little too vanilla for his palate. He hadn't bothered with a girl this white-bread since he first started. Besides, the police paid attention when girls like this disappeared. But . . . then again . . . He pushed up her eyelid and checked her sightless eyes. Dark irises. Dark hair, too. And the curve of her cheekbones spoke of something distinctly non-Aryan in her background. Could be part wetback or redskin, maybe even gook. His personal thirst—arousal, revulsion, and anger combined into an indistinguishable mélange—rose within him. She wasn't as tall or curvy as he usually liked them, but since she'd been so damn eager to get into his house, he would be willing to overlook her shortcomings. Of course, the basement wasn't furnished for more than one "guest," so he'd have to scavenge some substitute equipment from around the house. Hopefully she'd stay asleep until he found what he needed. Until then, he'd have to keep her locked up.

Leaving her meager belongings on the carpet (having labeled them "useless," his mind had already discarded all thought of them), he grabbed her by one arm and dragged her across the floor, all the while humming a happy tune. The door leading down to the basement was, like the outer door, triple bolted. He flipped each lock with his free hand, swung the door open, and pulled her to the top of the stairs. Then, still humming, he grabbed her by the shoulder and hip and flipped her over the edge.

Her limp form rolled down the steps, her arms and legs thumping against the wall and railing as they flopped erratically with the tumbling motion. One boot popped off her foot, bounced off the wall, and sailed out of sight as she fell.

With a final thump, her body landed at the foot of the stairs, face turned sideways, legs bent at the knee, and one arm pinned beneath her. She groaned again and flexed the fingers on one hand while twitching the foot of the opposite leg. He nodded approvingly. She survived the fall. Maybe she was tougher than she looked. Good. It was always more fun when they could take a lot of punishment.

He closed the door, bolted all three locks, and began his search for the particular items he would need.

OUTSIDE, IN THE backyard next door, a woman's brown coat reached one half-empty sleeve down into an open trash can. The inhuman hand inside the sleeve closed around a discarded cell phone.

TRAPPED

R achel awoke encased in cold darkness. Swimming in disorientation, she tried to realign her dizzy brain with her body, only to discover that her entire body ached and she was missing a boot. A faint smell—some sort of cleanser—stung her nose and sharpened her senses as she drew a deep breath.

Forcing her eyes to focus, she found that the room she was in was windowless and pitch black, except for a horizontal line of light several yards above her. *A door*, her mind finally grasped. The light was leaking under a door at the top of a staircase. *Oh shit*, she thought with a stab of raw terror. *I'm in the basement.*

She sat up and felt a crack of pain shoot through her. She grabbed her torso, wincing. The pain was coming from a spot just below her left breast. *Probably a fractured rib, maybe two.* Very slowly, she climbed to her feet and took note of every ache she felt. Her eyes gradually adjusted to the darkness, and she spotted her missing boot across the room. She limped across the floor to retrieve it, glancing around all the while.

The room, little more than a nine-by-nine cube, was empty. She grabbed her boot and then ran her hand along the wall. The rough texture of cinder blocks met her fingers, triggering a sinking sensation in her gut. There was no way she could bust through solid concrete. She looked up the stairs to the door connecting this little cell to the house. Squinting intently, she saw a series of faint metallic glints on the edge, just above the doorknob. Deadbolts, three of them—just like the exterior basement door. Hazy though her mind still was, she registered that this seemed like excessive protection for a basement, even for a guy who, like the oracle said, was paranoid. It could only mean that he was hiding something in here, and a guy like this didn't hide pleasant things. She reflexively reached for her coat pocket, only to find it empty. The severity of the situation sank in: she was in a violent man's well-protected basement, she was injured, her backup wouldn't arrive for who knew how long, and her phone was gone. A surge of fear electrified her veins and prickled through her skin.

"This can't be happening," she whispered to herself. "This cannot be fucking happening."

"Hey!" bellowed a muffled voice. "I hear you talking, dammit! Let me out of here, *now!*"

Rachel's eyes followed the sound and zeroed in on another door she hadn't previously noticed. It was tucked back, half-hidden by the stairs, and, like every other door Rachel had seen connected to this basement, secured by three deadbolts. This time, however, the locks were facing her. She shoved her foot into her boot, cringing from the pain in her sides as she did so, hobbled across the floor, unlocked the three bolts, and pulled the door toward her.

This room was even darker than the one Rachel was standing in; everything past the threshold was a curtain of pure black.

"Hello?" she called into the darkness. "Is someone here?"

"Who's that?" shouted a woman's voice. "Where are you?"

The voice was familiar. It confirmed the presence of a prisoner Rachel had already known was there.

"Miss Morley?" She limped through the doorway and paused, waiting in vain for her weary eyes to pierce the blackness. "Are you okay?"

"Fuck no, I'm not okay!" Miss Morley screamed. "Who are you?"

"I'm Rachel Wilde. I'm the one who gave you the flash drive."

There was a long silence. Guilty tension rippled up Rachel's arms and put the hair on the back of her neck on end.

"You led that bastard to me," Miss Morley hissed. "You set me up."

"No," Rachel said. "I needed the information on that flash drive to lead me to him. I didn't know he would come after you."

Rachel heard Miss Morley draw a breath—a tired, ragged, mortally terrified breath. Only then did she realize that the bravado and outrage in the woman's voice had been an act. Leda Morley might put up a front tougher than a bulletproof vest, but underneath that front she was deathly afraid.

"Why are you here?" Miss Morley asked quietly.

"I'm supposed to arrest him."

"Arrest him?" The doubt in her voice suggested she might more readily believe that Rachel was the Tooth Fairy come to track down an errant molar. "*You* came here to arrest *him*?"

"Yeah . . ." Rachel sighed. "I'm not doing a very good job. But don't worry, I have backup on the way. They'll be here soon."

"You're a cop?"

"No."

"Then what?"

"It's . . . complicated."

Rachel put one hand on the wall and slowly walked toward Miss Morley's voice. Never in her life had she been so uncomfortable with the absence of light. The passage that separated her house from the rest of the world was far darker than this basement, and yet it wasn't nearly as menacing. The passage to the pocket dimension was a snippet of nothingness, just two steps' worth of void. The emptiness of that dimensional gateway triggered a spasm in her senses and a nervous dread in her spirit, but the physical response she felt now was far more primal. The darkness here concealed things, secret and horrible things. She was a mouse trapped in a snake's hole, and the animal instinct inside her cowered at the reptilian air she breathed.

Something thin and cold suddenly brushed her cheek. She shrieked, jumped back, and blindly struck the wall, gaining herself a fresh bruise. The pain in her ribs flared up and constricted her lungs. She hissed through her teeth and crouched low to the ground, willing her heartbeat to slow. Anger and self-reproach quickly displaced her fear. *Being trapped like a mouse is no excuse for acting like one.*

Despite the fire in her side, she stood up and inched forward, waving one arm in front of her to find the offending object. Her fingers closed around it, and she found it to be long, thin, and made up of tiny plastic links. A possible explanation popped into her head, and she gripped it in her hand and pulled.

A lone bulb over her head clicked on and cast its urine-colored light over the room.

This room was slightly larger than the last—about twelve by twelve—but like that room, it was solid concrete, and as uniformly gray as an overcast sky. There were a few cracks in the floor, accompanied by a couple of dark stains that showed signs of recent scrubbing. The odor of cleanser she had smelled in the other room was stronger here, as was her sense of foreboding. Nevertheless, with the darkness removed, the primitive fear in Rachel's gut diminished and her training kicked in. Mind focused, she turned and approached her fellow captive.

Leda Morley's swollen, bloody cheek was the first thing Rachel saw. The second was the iron restraint, connected to the cinder block wall by a short but thick chain, that was binding her wrist.

Mindful of the chain but focusing on one issue at a time, she made a quick assessment of Miss Morley's condition. Aside from her cheek, she showed no obvious signs of injury. Her clothes were ripped and stained, probably from their owner being stuffed into and pulled out of a footlocker, but what she could see of her skin appeared intact. Rachel got closer and saw that there was a large smear of blood on Miss Morley's lower lip and chin although her lips were not split and there was no blood around her nostrils.

"You didn't lose a tooth, did you?" she asked. "I see blood on your mouth."

"It's his," said Leda. "I bit him."

Rachel raised an eyebrow and nodded approvingly. "You did better than I did. Do you have any other injuries?"

"My neck hurts from getting bumped around in that trunk, but I'm okay." She jostled the chain holding her wrist. "Can you get this damn thing off me?"

Rachel seized the chain and pulled it as hard as her injuries would allow, but it was unshakably anchored to the wall. She stuck her hand in her coat pocket, but, not surprisingly, her lockpick was missing. She shook her head.

"It's on there tight."

This news clearly did not surprise Miss Morley, but it brought a tremble to her lip and a tear to her eye. She bowed her head and folded her hands under her chin. "Oh God," she moaned. "Jesus, please save me."

The sight of Miss Morley praying made Rachel uncomfortable. Religion was an uncommon thing among her people, and those who had it kept it private. More to the point, however, praying struck Rachel as being an unproductive use of time and energy under the circumstances. She turned and scanned the room for anything that might be a help to them.

She saw two locked doors. The three deadbolts on one were accessible, but also accompanied by a fourth lock, a formidable padlock. She flipped the three deadbolts and gave the knob a shake. The padlock did its job and held the door firmly in place.

Cursing, she pulled the knob as hard as she could, and a faint sliver of light became visible through the edge. *That's the light by the driveway,* she deduced. *This is the door that leads outside.* Her fractured ribs cried out and she released the knob, whereupon the door clicked back into place, swallowing her glimpse of freedom.

She crossed the basement and approached the other door. This door had no deadbolts, but like the door to the driveway, it had a padlock. The door jiggled a little when Rachel yanked it, but the padlock held. She planted her feet and pulled as hard as she could until it yielded up a paper-thin view of the far side. Still straining against the lock, she peeked through the opening. The inside was shallow, like a closet, and from within, something metal reflected the light of the lone bulb behind her. She tried to lean a little closer to see the source of the glint, but as she did so, the stench of bleach struck her like a wave of mustard gas. Gagging, eyes watering, she released the door, but not before she caught the faint trace of an odor under the bleach. *What is that rancid stink?* she thought, her stomach churning. *Spoiled meat?* Whatever it was, she wanted no part of it. She moved away from the closet and determined not to touch it again.

Rachel looked around the empty room again. Aside from the locked doors, the only other opening was a tiny vent on the ceiling. Her stomach knotted and her heart climbed into her throat. There was no way out and nothing she could use as a tool to help them escape. With mounting panic, Rachel grabbed Leda's wrist restraint again and, ignoring her body's wails of pain, pulled with all her weight. Miss Morley also grabbed the chain, planted one bare foot against the wall, and added her strength to the effort. Together, the two women pulled with all their combined force, but the rods that held the chain to the wall did not budge. They loosed their grip and dropped the chain, panting.

"That fucker's not going anywhere," Miss Morley spat.

"There's blood on it," Rachel suddenly said. She scraped some reddish flakes from the edge with her fingernail. "See here, right by your wrist."

"Are you sure it's blood?"

"Yeah," she said reluctantly. "I'm sure."

"Well . . ." Miss Morley whispered. "It's not mine."

But it's someone's, Rachel thought. *Someone was in this re-*

straint before Miss Morley. He's brought someone else down here before . . . maybe more than one "someone else." Maybe—the knot in her stomach twisted—*that's what the nasty stink in the closet is about. Maybe that spoiled meat smell is . . .*

The expression on Miss Morley's face told Rachel that the two of them were reaching the same dreadful conclusion.

Seeing her own horror reflected back at her, Miss Morley closed her eyes, dropped to her knees, and turned her face up toward the ceiling. She clasped her hands under her chin and kept her lips moving in prayer even as she forced back the tears that filled her eyes. "Jesus, please help me," she prayed. "Please, please help me!"

Rachel paced the room with her hands pressed to her screaming ribs as she desperately assessed the situation. The plastic chain on the light bulb was too flimsy and too short to choke a man. The padlock on the door would make a good weapon, but it was attached to the wall. It seemed like all she could do at this point was wait for Wu to show up, although knowing he was the closest to arriving did not alleviate her fear. Wu was decent at hand-to-hand fighting, but, truthfully, he was not any better than she was. In a fight between Wu and her captor, she would have to bet on the latter. Suarez was a much better bet. He was Hallan, born and raised in a warrior society; he could take down a psycho like this without breaking a sweat. But he was farther away than Wu, and at this point there was no telling how long it would be before he got there. There had to be another option. There had to be a way out. If there wasn't . . .

Her eyes darted to the foul closet and she shivered. This man had overpowered her easily when she was rested and un-hurt; now she was exhausted, in pain, sporting a possible concussion, and locked in a basement. She didn't have her cell phone, she didn't have her lockpick, she didn't have a weapon. The only advantage she'd ever had on the guy was—

"What was on the flash drive?"

Miss Morley raised her head and stared at Rachel with bloodshot, defeated eyes. "What?"

"The flash drive I gave you. What was on it?"

Leda's brow furrowed and she shook her head. "What the hell does it matter?"

"It might matter a lot," Rachel pressed. "The only advantage I have on this guy is that I know what he's been up to for the last few months and he doesn't realize it. Just tell me: Did you learn anything from that memory stick?"

Miss Morley sighed. She drew her knees up to her chest and wrapped her unfettered arm around them. "The few sections I had time to translate looked like diary entries."

Rachel blinked and cocked her head. "Diaries?"

"They're descriptions of people's lives: births, deaths, marriages, daily occupations, and other personal business, not all of which I could translate clearly." Miss Morley raised her hands in a gesture of helpless frustration. "They are hundreds, maybe even thousands, of years old, but they're very mundane. They might be interesting for a historian, but to the average person they'd be pretty damn boring."

Stunned, Rachel thought of the long list of files on the flash drive. They were all diaries? How could that be? "All those different documents in all those different languages . . ." She shook her head incredulously. "They were just personal journals?"

"I just got started on them, but yeah, so far that's it."

Rachel frowned. "Then why did he want the drive so badly?

Why did he go to the trouble of tracking it down if that's all there is? It doesn't make sense."

"Sense?" Miss Morley thrust her pointer finger in Rachel's direction, jangling the chain as she shook her arm. "You're trying to make sense out of this? We're in a murderer's basement!"

"I noticed!" Rachel snapped back. She winced and grabbed her ribs again. She spoke again, this time calmer. "I'm saying there's something missing, something I'm not seeing." She chewed on her lower lip and let the events of the day whirl through her mind. One item at a time, they dropped away, discarded for being irrelevant. Soon, there was nothing left. Pissed at her own seemingly useless brain, she gritted her teeth and balled her fists. "There *must be* something."

"I'm telling you, there's not," Miss Morley said, her voice underscored by fear. "It's all crap. It's got nothing to do with keeping girls chained in a basement!" On the last syllable of this sentence, Miss Morley's voice broke and long-withheld tears burst from her eyes. She sniffled and buried her face in her knees. Even as she wept, however, she kept her lips tight to muffle the sound of her cries, as if by keeping them in she was stopping her strength from leaking out of her body.

The almost inaudible sounds pecked at Rachel's heart. *It's my fault she's here.* Thoroughly exhausted, mentally and physically, she slid down the wall and sat next to Miss Morley. She put an arm around the woman's shoulders and gave her a gentle hug. "I have two friends on their way here," she said. "They'll get us out."

"If he doesn't kill us before then," Miss Morley rasped. "Sweet Jesus, help me."

Laden with guilt, Rachel ventured another squeeze and pressed her cheek to Miss Morley's hair. After a few more muffled sobs, the young woman raised her head, threw her one free arm around Rachel, and resumed crying.

Despite the pain in her ribs, Rachel put both arms around Miss Morley and held her. In between sobs, the young woman prayed and clutched at Rachel's coat with trembling fingers. Rachel held her tight but didn't offer any assurances. Instead, she just held on, waited, and, against all reasonable expectation, hoped.

Give me something, she begged of no one in particular. *Something,* anything. *Give me a string to grasp at and I'll turn it into garrote. Give me a rock and I'll turn it into a hammer. Give me a pin and I'll gouge out his eyes. Just. Give. Me.* Something.

The two women held each other as the seconds ticked away, each one bringing them closer to a confrontation with their captor and, probably, the end of their lives. Leda prayed for the cuff to crumble off her wrist and for the door to open. Rachel silently begged for a weapon to fall into her hand and for Wu and Suarez to show up ahead of schedule.

Neither of them got what they asked for.

What they did get was the sudden appearance of Rachel's cell phone, glasses, card, and lockpick at their feet.

WASTELAND

L eda Morley had first seen her lace-trimmed blue skirt in the window of a boutique and had loved it so much that she'd decided at first sight that she would buy it. She had purchased the white knit top she was wearing to replace a similar one that had not survived a bad date at an Italian restaurant. She wasn't particularly attached to it but it was versatile, so it had made its way into her regular wardrobe rotation. That ninety-dollar skirt was now stained with black splotches and torn up the side. The top, meanwhile, had a ragged hole the size of a fist in it, just above her belly button, and was smeared with grime. The dark blue blazer she'd bought on sale last fall was missing a sleeve, ripped from its seams when her captor dragged her out of the footlocker. Her shoes, blue pumps that were classy and comfortable, were gone.

As for the body underneath the clothes—uncountable strands of hair had been pulled from her head, mostly from contact with the footlocker but also when the kidnapper grabbed her by the hair. That was when she bit him; he couldn't have known that she had paid handsomely for a perm just two days earlier, a price she paid regularly in order to maintain her "professional" appearance. She could still taste his coppery blood on her teeth. Her wounded cheek was throbbing, her head and neck hurt, she was drained, she was cold, and she desperately wanted to hear her mother's voice.

She didn't understand who Rachel Wilde was or how she had ended up in this basement with her, but she was too frightened to dislike her or question her motives. If she was going to die in this psycho's basement, then she would clutch at any comfort she had, even if it came from a strange woman who was clearly not who she had pretended to be. The presence of a fellow victim was a sick sort of comfort, but it was comfort nonetheless, and with the shadow of death creeping over her, she could not pick and choose her blessings. So she held tight to Rachel and, entirely against her nature, cried freely.

And then the cell phone and other items fell to the floor like manna from Heaven.

Already on edge, Leda jumped and clutched at Rachel with one hand while flailing the other, cutting her wrist on the metal cuff clasped around it in the process. She hardly felt the pain over her fright as fresh blood oozed over that left by the previous victim and created a new, larger red stain.

Heart racing, she scanned the room, expecting to see their captor in every shadow. Finding no one else in the room, her eyes fell to the things on the floor. Because of her crazed panic, it took a moment for her to understand what she was seeing. But once her brain embraced what was in front of her eyes, she was so struck with excitement and relief that she didn't give a damn where it had come from.

"A phone!" she shouted. She slapped a hand over her mouth, her startled eyes darting to the ceiling. "Oh God," she whispered. "I hope he didn't hear me."

Rachel snatched up her things. "Did you see him?" she asked.

For a moment, Leda wondered what she was talking about, but then she realized she wasn't speaking to her. She followed Rachel's gaze but saw nothing but a crumpled old coat. The woman was talking to air.

"Who are you talking to?" Leda asked.

Rachel didn't respond. She continued staring into nothing, listening to silence. Terror mounting, Leda grabbed Rachel's arm and jostled her, but the other woman's eyes stayed locked on the coat. She was trying to decide what to do about this insanity when Rachel suddenly shook off her hand, picked up a twisted, pronged length of metal, and attacked Leda's wrist restraint.

Leda instantly forgave her companion's strange behavior as she watched her work, filled with hope. She stayed as still as possible, though her muscles twitched with anxious energy. The fact that Rachel continued to glance back, still listening intently to the air, disturbed her, but if she could get the cuff off her arm, she would overlook this sudden display of irrationality.

"Where is he now?" Rachel asked the air. "What's he doing? Really? Unbelievable. Hmm? What's that?" Rachel's eyes darted to Leda, startling her. "What about her?" she said over her shoulder. "How do you know?"

The cuff popped open and Leda's bleeding wrist fell free. Her heart leapt. Whispering a breathless thank-you to Jesus and his father, she jumped to her feet, ran across the frigid concrete surface to the driveway door, and jerked the knob. The padlock held firm.

She turned to Rachel. "Can you open this one, too?"

But Rachel wasn't listening. Her entire attention was held by the same thing she had been looking at since the reappearance of her belongings: the coat.

Faced with this inexplicable behavior in a time of extreme crisis, Leda's heart thundered, a raucous beat driven by anger and fear. She lunged for Rachel, grabbed her by the arm, and shook her.

"Snap out of it!" she said. "He could come down here any minute!"

"Stop!" Rachel snapped, yanking her arm out of Leda's grasp. "He won't be coming down here for a while. He dug a bunch of rope out of his attic, and now the freak's eating dinner."

"How the hell do you know that?"

"The daemon told me."

Leda opened her mouth to respond, but no words came to her. Her brow furrowed and she shook her head. Rachel's statement raised more questions than she was prepared to ask. Before she could decide which question was most worthy, Rachel whipped out her glasses and slipped them on. Her brown eyes, strangely distorted by the lenses, grew wide as they swept over the room.

"Shit," she said. "It's everywhere."

Leda stared, mouth agape, at Rachel. Her eyes darted to the door, and then back to Rachel again. "*What* is everywhere? What the hell is with you?"

"He's been trying to punch a hole right here," she said. "The signs are all over this place. Oh shit . . . this is so far out of my league."

The adrenaline in Leda's blood pushed her patience beyond its limit. This woman had brought her the flash drive that led to her abduction, she had conveniently reappeared in time to join Leda in this dungeon, and now she was talking to the air and refusing to open the door that would free them. *What the fuck?* Leda's jaw clenched and she balled her fists so tight that her broken fingernails cut into her skin.

"I don't know what the fuck is wrong with you, bitch," she said in a low voice, fresh tears welling up in her eyes, "but if you don't open that goddamn door, I'm gonna—"

Rachel took off the glasses and, quick as a snap, popped them on Leda's face.

It took all her resolve not to scream.

Through the lenses, the gray room suddenly became a wash of outlandish color. Frantic patterns swirled and flared in a mist that covered everything in sight, including her own body. Pink, misty spikes rose from the ground, each one six feet tall and mired in an orange bog that covered the entire floor, corner to corner, wall to wall. The bog was riddled with a thousand fluttering, pulsing veins. Black spiral spots appeared and disappeared in the orange goo like winking monster eyes.

Choking on a cry, Leda instinctively backed away from the sight, only to back into the wall restraint that was streaked with her blood.

"W-what?" she sputtered. "What?"

"Don't freak out," said Rachel's voice beside her. "It can't hurt you."

Terror paralyzed Leda. The alien phantasms she saw through the glasses compounded her already extreme fear of the basement and its owner. Fight or flight overloaded her heart until the pain in her chest left her gulping for breath. Her knees began to shake and slowly started to buckle.

Rachel grabbed her arm and hoisted her up. "Stay with

me," she said firmly. "It can't hurt you. Think of it as television: it's just an image."

"What is it?" Leda murmured, her eyes too wide to blink.

"What you're seeing," Rachel explained, "is someone's attempt to punch a hole in the dimensional spectrum. The orange signifies that the barrier between dimensions has been significantly weakened, and those pink towers are signs of violent death. My people can open passages between dimensions using technology that's common to us, but there are other ways to open an interdimensional passage that are more easily accessible to someone who's not from my homeland. One of those ways"—she flinched—"involves repeated torture and murder using . . . certain instruments. Probably what's in that closet." She nodded in the direction of the second padlocked door. "The black dots you see tell me that he's trying to open a passage to the daemon wasteland." She ran a hand through her hair, pulling it back from her forehead. "This psycho's been committing murder to open a passage to the wastes, and he's getting really close to succeeding."

Leda shuddered. "W-wastes?"

"It's where my people send defective daemons when their defect makes them dangerous and they can't be repaired. He's trying to set dangerous daemons loose in your world."

"Daemons?"

"Like the one that brought me my phone, glasses, and lockpick." She pointed to the spot she had been speaking to. "Look there."

Leda's eyes obediently dropped and there she found another blow to her already fragile state of mind. There, at Rachel's feet, she saw a squat, green monstrosity with wrinkly skin covering fatty folds and warty lumps. Black-and-pink claws protruded from feet beneath its round stomach, and more tipped the fingers on its meaty hands. A curly, cord-like appendage she couldn't identify stuck out of the creature's right side at a downward angle, and undulating rolls of skin rippled over its body. The monster had a bulging eye, four pointed ears, and a tooth-filled mouth that wrapped halfway around its head. It looked vacantly at Leda with its trollish face, as if it hardly noticed that she was there. Then it turned its back to her, gathered its coat around itself, and waddled across the glowing floor, dragging the tails of the coat behind it, to the far wall, where it passed through a cinder block and disappeared from sight like it had never existed at all.

Leda clapped a hand over her gaping mouth. Suddenly light-headed, she felt her legs start to give. Rachel snatched the glasses off her face, and instantly the concrete dungeon was colorless again. Leda heaved an enormous breath and her body flooded with relief.

"I'm sorry," Rachel said. "I'm sorry I sprang that on you, but I didn't have time for a lengthy explanation that you weren't prepared to believe." She brushed past Leda, lockpick in hand, and went to work on the driveway door padlock. "I'm gonna get you out of here, but you need to understand this: you can't call anyone once we're out."

Despite still feeling off-balance from what she had just seen, Leda whirled on Rachel. "What?" she said, stunned and outraged. "Are you crazy?"

"What this guy's up to," Rachel told her over her shoulder, "your laws don't cover. Ours do."

"And the blood on that cuff? The blood that's *not* mine?"

"He'll be held accountable for that too. And he'll be held accountable for your abduction. And," she added irritably, "he'll be held accountable for clocking me in the head." She huffed, shook her head, and muttered, "Twice."

"He kidnapped me," Leda said through clenched teeth. "He locked me up down here to do God knows what to me and . . . and I don't know what's going on with those crazy-ass glasses, but it can't be good. Do you seriously think I'm not going to call the police on that fucker?"

"If you do, what's to stop him from doing this again?" Rachel countered. "If he got his hands on the right tools once, odds are he can do it again. And even if he goes to prison— always a big *if* in your society—all he has to do is bribe someone to get the necessary instrument, and then he can start over. There's no shortage of people to murder in prison, right? I told you, your people aren't equipped for this. Mine are."

She yanked the lock; it didn't open. She clenched her jaw and attacked it again.

"I'm gonna get us out, and then I'm gonna wait for my backup. With their help, I'll finally be able to arrest this sicko. Just . . . just don't call the cops, okay?" She glanced over her shoulder at Leda, her hands still working on the lock without the aid of her eyes. "Okay? Just go home and let me do my job. Please?"

Leda locked eyes with the woman before her and saw something foreign in her stare, something almost as alien as the green monster she had seen walk through the mist. It wasn't the first time she'd seen that look in someone's eyes (she saw it often enough in the eyes of tourists at the museum who were hundreds of miles from home), but never before had she seen one of this depth. Rachel Wilde, whoever she was, was a long way from her home and a long way from her "normal." Leda thought again of what she had seen through the glasses, and it made her shudder. That "normal" was a far cry from her own, much farther than any "normal" should be.

She put a shaky hand over her bruised cheek, took a deep breath, and exhaled slowly. "I don't understand what's happening here," she said. "I think maybe that psycho hit me harder than I thought and all this is some trauma-induced nightmare. I'm going to wake up in a hospital with my mama sitting next to me, and after I get a long night's sleep, I'm going to go back to work and forget all about this shit."

"Sounds good to me," Rachel said just as the lock popped open, so quickly that it startled both women.

Rachel whipped it off the latch, hooked two fingers through the open loop, and tucked it against her palm. "You go home and sleep until tonight isn't real anymore. I'll take this freak into custody, and you'll never have to see him or me ever again. Now let's get out of here."

Rachel grabbed the knob and pulled. The heavy door flew open much faster than it should have—too fast for the amount of force Rachel had used to open it. It struck her in the shoulder, shoving her back. Her elbow hit Leda in the chest and knocked her against the wall. Rachel reeled but kept her feet. The blow to Leda's chest knocked the wind out of her, but she didn't fall either. They were both standing when the owner of the house walked through the doorway, tossed a coil of rope and a roll of duct tape to the floor, and calmly closed the door behind him, locking the bolts.

"Don't know how you got through the locks, girls," he said in an oh-so-pleasant voice, "but you're not leaving." He held up his hands and gestured around the concrete room. "This is your home now. But don't worry," he added through a smile that would make a wolf cower, "you won't be staying long."

15

RIOT

The yellowish light of the lone basement bulb cast a sickly mask of shadows over the man's face that made his toothy smile look unnaturally bright, like a dragon's mouth lit from fire within. Animal alarm exploded through Rachel's body; since there was nowhere to run, she balled her fists and prepared to fight.

"Why are you doing this?" Rachel demanded.

"I can do what I want," he said. "I don't need a reason."

"Why would you want to punch a hole in the dimensional spectrum?" she yelled. "And why to the wastes?"

The man looked at her in speechless surprise, his thin mouth slightly agape. For a brief moment, his composure slipped. But he quickly pulled himself together and flashed his snakelike smile.

"You're from that other place, aren't you?" he said with the air of a king addressing a lowly peasant. "When I saw you upstairs, I thought you were just a common mongrel, some sort of mulatto whore with your muddy skin, but I get it now. You're one of those people who fixes the demons. They warned me that someone like you might show up eventually. Messing with the 'natural order' always brings out people like you, according to them."

Rachel stared. Her arms trembled and her whole body felt surreally cold. "What is it you know?"

"I know you're from another layer," he said with a smirk. "The people I talked to called it another color in the 'spectrum rainbow.'"

Rachel's pupils contracted slightly at the word. Rainbow. She remembered teachers and instructors using that word repeatedly during her education. The human dimensional spectrum is like a rainbow, they said, with each color containing a layer of reality. It was a reference any Arcanan would recognize. But this man was Notan. The owner of the dungeon grinned in self-satisfaction at the sight of her shock.

"They said they can't use their own technology because too many people would notice, so they have to resort to messier methods. They brought me into their fold because I can perform the tasks that they can't, since they have to stay hidden." He leaned toward the women just a bit, his cold eyes gleaming with reptilian avarice. "They need me, you see."

Rachel did not see. She did not understand what was happening. Her Arcanan-born, Arcanan-bred, Arcanan-raised mind could not fathom that this psychopath had been hired by her own people to do something that went against everything her world believed in. It was illogical . . . and sick. It was . . . un-Arcanan.

LEDA HAD NO such cultural barrier to overcome, and though she didn't fully understand what was happening, she knew a narcissistic sack of shit when she saw one. In that way, this man reminded her of her boss, and she had never once been afraid of that asshole. Seeing her captor in this new light, she gained courage.

"I see," she said, scanning the man from head to toe. Her nose wrinkled and she shook her head. "You're just some dumb bastard who's doing some other dumb bastard's dirty work. Dumbest thing about it is they're just using you but you still think you're important." She snorted and pursed her lips. "Fuckwit."

This assault on his intelligence stirred the would-be placid waters of his expression, but he visibly forced his anger into check. Leda saw the impact of her words, and she suppressed a smile.

He clenched his jaw and flashed his teeth in a smile that was like a crocodile's grimace. "I'm not as dumb as you'd like to think," he said, sneering. "I know who you are. They said I would find you somewhere in this city, so I've been poring over the journals to figure out where you were hiding. I really had to dig deep, in the journals and in the public record, but I knew I was close. I didn't think I'd pick you up purely by chance, but the phone call I just got confirmed it—I've got you." He grinned hungrily at the center of the dungeon floor, at the old stains that had escaped the bleach. "The blood of those other girls I picked up would have eventually done the trick, but it's been slow going. Your blood, on the other hand . . ." He sighed happily. "Oh, that should really make an impact. I don't know if the gate will open with your blood alone, but even if it doesn't, I'll bet it makes one hell of a dent. And now that I know who you are, I can hunt down the rest of the women in your family. Once they're all dead, Apep will pass over to this dimension by default. And I'll just bet he leaves a nasty gash in the dimensional boundary when he does."

He giggled like a child—a disconcerting, unnatural sound. Leda was beyond hope of grasping all of his babble, but his fixation on her, her blood, and her family renewed her fear and rendered her silent. She shot a look at Rachel, hoping for an explanation, but on her face she saw only shock.

RACHEL TURNED ONE disbelieving eye to Miss Morley. "You're the gatekeeper?" she whispered. When Leda only stared blankly at her in response, she shook her head. "The daemon said it saw something strange in you but . . . I didn't know."

Rachel looked at Miss Morley as if for the first time. This couldn't be real; and even if it could, it shouldn't be. The odds against stumbling upon the missing gatekeeper while tracking down a mark from a completely different case were astronomical. There was no coincidence broad enough to cover this situation. Except . . . an oracle had led her here. When an oracle read the map, even the most divergent paths would eventually cross. Bach had, without actively knowing it, brought these two paths to a junction, the crossroads at which she now stood. To the right, a psycho trying to open a portal to the daemon wastes. To the left, the last scion of an ancient gatekeeper line, the extinction of which would open just such a portal. These two should never have met and would not have if not for the oracle . . . and Rachel herself.

"Ladies, take a seat against the wall," their captor said, pointing at the chain and cuff dangling from the concrete. "Sit down, stay still, and we'll get started."

"Up yours," Rachel snarled.

"Are you under the impression that you have a choice?" he asked. His eager, pleasant expression suddenly hardened into a visage of hateful monstrosity. His lip curled back from his teeth like a rabid dog's and his eyes filled with lightning. In seconds, the tranquil man with a song on his lips had dropped the mask that camouflaged the near-soulless truth within. He glared viciously at Rachel and pointed at the wall again. "Put your ass on the floor, you dumb bitch, or I'll put it there for you."

When Rachel didn't move, his nostrils flared and he took a step in her direction.

"Don't you get it, whore?" he snapped. "I already beat your ass once today." He took another step, thrusting his face inches from hers so that she could smell turkey and mustard on his breath. "Are you stupid or just a masochist? I'll take you apart and scatter the pieces of your body all over the city, just like I did to those other girls, and no one will ever kn—"

Rachel swung at him, and for the first time made contact. The heavy padlock in her hand struck the man in the side of the head just shy of his left eye. He reeled and staggered backward a few steps while trying to catch his balance. Rachel rushed forward and hit him again, in the back of the head this time, knocking him to the floor. She leapt on top of him and starting twisting his ear with her other hand while hitting him about the head with the lock.

"Run!" she shouted to Miss Morley. "Go!"

With a startled gasp, the other woman darted around the fallen man and lunged for the door. She flipped the locks, turned the knob, and yanked, but only managed to expose a sliver of light before her stunned captor's flailing legs caught her in the knee. Rachel heard something pop out of place, and Miss Morley shrieked in pain as her leg buckled beneath her.

The man swung his foot again, and this time connected with the door, which banged shut. Before Miss Morley could steady herself, he was kicking again at her knee, even as he grabbed a fistful of Rachel's hair and yanked her off of his back.

Miss Morley fell to the floor, screaming with blind pain.

HE CONTINUED TO kick at the museum bitch, trying to aim for joints and soft spots to inflict the maximum amount of damage, while simultaneously trying to put enough distance between himself and his attacker to land a serious blow.

The smaller girl was clinging to him doggedly, one arm wrapped around his neck while the other pounded away at him with the padlock, coming agonizingly close to fracturing his skull. By pure luck, he grabbed her wrist and managed to pry the lock out of her fingers. She surprised him by immediately using her newly freed hand to secure her hold around his neck. He expected her to go to pieces with her weapon gone, but instead she kept a level head and continued her attack undaunted. It was just what he would have done in her place, and that shocked him. By the time he recovered from his amazement, she was already choking him.

He turned his head just in time to see the other woman crawling toward the discarded padlock. Snarling, he heaved himself up, with his attacker still choking him from behind, and flung his body backward against the cinder block wall.

The girl threw her head forward far enough to avoid another knock to her skull, but he felt the blow snuff all the air from her lungs. She gasped, breathless, and he took advantage of her helpless state to rip free from her arms and fling her, still desperate for air, to the floor. Then he marched to the museum woman, kicked the padlock out of her reach, and stomped on her outstretched hand. He heard a snap; she began to scream again. Unbothered by her pain, he seized her by the wrist and dragged her, kicking and clawing, to the far side of the room, where he dropped her against the wall, right next to Rachel.

"Stay there!" he bellowed.

He could feel the blood matting in his graying hair and running down his face. Panting, he turned his back to his captives, snatched up the padlock, and marched to the basement door.

"Goddamned bitches," he said hoarsely, massaging his bruised throat. "I'm sticking to one at a time from now—"

The door was open. He stared at it in astonishment. His memory of the last few minutes was a bit jumbled, but he was very sure that he had stopped the museum bitch from opening the door. He glanced back at his captives; they were just where he'd left them, still too shaken and wounded to move. He quickly closed the door and reattached the padlock. That done, he felt a delightful sense of routine wash over him. The empty smile returned to his lips. The girls were back under his control. Now he could begin.

He turned toward them with a ready-made speech on his tongue. He would tell them, as he'd told the others, what awaited them. He would bind them and then unlock the closet to introduce them to his many blood-seasoned tools, one at a time. Most girls didn't live long enough to meet the last few instruments (the "corkscrew" in particular), but these two were stronger than most; despite the disappointments of the last few minutes, he had high hopes for them.

Smiling eagerly, he took a step toward them—the usual introductory speech taking shape in his mind—only to be distracted by a shadow at his feet. He glanced down and squinted in puzzlement.

There was a ratty brown coat on the floor.

"Bitch must have dropped it earlier," he mumbled as he leaned down to pick it up.

The coat darted away from his fingers. He was startled to see a piece of clothing move, but he was also instinctively annoyed to see it attempt to evade him. Without thinking, he sprang forward and grabbed the sleeve.

The coat lurched and covered his hand, and a pain like he had never felt before exploded through his arm. He let fly an agonized, terrified scream that shook the concrete walls. It was as if a box of invisible red-hot pins had invaded his hand and burst through his veins and muscles on their way up his arm, leaving a hundred smoldering tunnels in their wake. He yanked his arm back, but the coat stayed with him, clinging to him with its unseen teeth. He wildly flung his arm this way and that to shake it loose. Droplets of his blood struck the floor, walls, and ceiling, but the coat did not let go.

He tucked the coat to his side, pinned the previously unnoticed bulk with his arm, and pulled his hand free. Long strips of his skin and flesh ripped away with the coat, but with the pain of the bite still coursing through his arm, he could hardly feel it. He hurled the coat in the direction of the two girls and gasped for breath as he tried and failed to flex his fingers. He looked over at the coat; the strips of skin torn from his hand dangled from its collar like wet noodles, dripping blood down its buttons.

"What the fuck is that thing?" he shrieked.

RACHEL HAD NEVER seen a daemon bite anyone before, and in fact hadn't known for sure that it was possible until now, but she was thrilled to see it happen to her captor. She glanced at Miss Morley and saw a similar rush of excitement on her face. But quickly, very quickly, Miss Morley's expression shifted from a soft hope to a hard fury. Rachel had only a moment to puzzle about the sudden switch, because she suddenly felt a change come over her as well. The pain of her injuries dimmed as anger boiled in her blood and radiated through her, from her heart to the very tips of her fingers.

As the rage engulfed her, she glanced at the blood-spattered coat and understood. A riot daemon's function was to stir discord and incite violence. Its unheard whispers urged anyone with a grudge to react disproportionately, whether with words, gestures, or fists, and Rachel and Miss Morley had more than a simple grudge. Their blood was already warm from the struggle a minute ago, and now, with some intensive daemonic urging, it was searing hot.

Rachel flashed a smile at the coat that quickly and willingly became a snarl. She understood what was happening and she fully embraced it. Without hesitation, she stood up and launched herself at her captor. Despite the obvious damage to her knee, Miss Morley somehow did the same. Together, without pain, sense, or plan, they attacked their captor with fists, nails, and teeth, and with every adrenaline-driven ounce of strength their bodies could summon. They shrieked like mindless banshees through it all, but Rachel didn't even hear the mad voices as their own. The rage, the riot, consumed them both.

SHORT THE USE of his wounded arm and reeling from the pain, he could barely hold them off. The two defeated victims had suddenly and inexplicably transformed into rampaging harpies, and he couldn't wrap his mind around the change. Flashes of light and dark skin darted in and out of his vision, accompanied by stings and cracks. He fended them off with his one functioning arm, but unlike him they seemed to feel nothing and did not react to his counterblows. Their yowling mouths set his ears ringing, and he tried to shut them up, but every time he struck one in the teeth, she clamped her jaws on his fingers.

It took only seconds for them to take him to the floor. Once he was down, they crouched over him and continued their attack, and all he could do was blindly flail his arm at them.

At last, a lucky kick knocked one into the other and disoriented the pair long enough for him to scramble to the door. With only one functional hand, he was unable to unlock the padlock. He dodged the scrambling girls and ran for the stairs. As he passed into the basement anteroom, he flung the dividing door shut behind him and bolted the locks. Both women slammed their bodies against the door, sending a huge shock through the hinges. They screamed with inhuman voices and beat their fists on the slab.

He backed away, out of breath and wide-eyed. With his heart racing (a sensation he was unused to), he climbed the stairs toward the main level of his house.

With each step, he discovered a new ache or bloody gash. He was forced to gasp for air through his mouth, as his nose was smashed to bits, and in between each breath, he had to swallow down a mouthful of blood—one of the girls had knocked a tooth loose from his gums. His eyes returned again and again to his tattered arm as he struggled with the idea that the old coat had bitten him. As he neared the top step, he shook his head decisively.

"I'm calling the others about this," he said, thinking aloud. "There's something extremely wrong happening here." He reached the door, fumbled for the key in his pocket, and clumsily unlocked the bolts with one shaky hand. "Better to let them sort it out before I go back down."

More tired than he had been in years, he gingerly pushed open the door and let it swing casually into the kitchen. He stepped up onto the tile and, a second too late, realized that someone else was in the room.

Had he not been nursing his injuries and spinning in a whirlwind of thought, he would have sensed the intruder long before opening the door, but as it was, he was caught off guard, and the tall, skinny stranger successfully landed a punch right between his eyes.

Staggering blindly, he swiped his good arm at the assailant but made no contact. A hand grabbed him by the shirt and shoved him hard. He tripped over his own foot and fell backward down the very staircase he had just climbed. He surrendered his consciousness halfway down the steps.

WHEN WU UNBOLTED and opened the door, Rachel and Miss Morley burst into the anteroom. When she saw their captor bloody and unconscious on the floor, Rachel almost immediately felt the last of her strength leave her. Miss Morley seemed to be experiencing the same feeling, since she immediately slumped down the wall with a grunt and a sigh.

Already feeling her headache return with a vengeance, Rachel groaned wearily in the face of her rescuer. "Don't think I'm not glad to see you," she said in Arcanan, "but it sure took you long enough."

"Don't blame me for this freak," Wu said. "Blame the Central Office for misclassifying this case."

"As soon as they open their doors again, I will." As the last of the adrenaline trembled its way out of her body, she sighed and accepted the arm her friend was offering her. "Thanks, Wu."

He grinned his jokester grin, the endearing one that showed a few too many of his teeth.

"Not a problem. Hey, since I helped you out here, maybe you can pick up one of my assignments for this week. Shouldn't be a problem for you, right?"

Too tired to laugh and too bruised to reply, Rachel held her head in her hand and listened to the comforting sound of her own beating heart.

GATEKEEPER

Leda prodded her bandaged, splinted knee and winced. Patellar dislocation, according to the doctor. In other words, a dislocated kneecap. Tests showed no muscular or nerve damage—something of a miracle, considering the level of trauma she had suffered. Treatment: immobilization, crutches, and maybe surgery to repair ligament and arterial damage. Long-term outlook: rehabilitation would probably give her full or close to full mobility, but a lifetime of chronic pain and recurring dislocations were a distinct possibility.

Leda puffed a breath through a frown. Just a week ago she had paid for another year at the gym and signed up for a charity 5K at her church. The damage to her knee made the two broken bones in her left hand, the stitched-up gash on her cheek, and her chipped front tooth seem pretty trifling by comparison. She caught herself wallowing in self-pity and shook it off. She was alive; that was all that mattered. Next Sunday, she would take her name off the charity run sign-up, bow her head, and thank God that her mother wasn't identifying her remains at the morgue. That was worth the price of an unusable gym membership.

The doctor was talking to Rachel in a language Leda was

•

sure she had never heard before. Exhausted and traumatized though she was, her years of language study kicked in, compelling her to listen to the talk and try to parse out the grammatical structure of the alien sentences. Rachel was also listening attentively, but her eyes looked heavy and her shoulders were bowed as if the full weight of the day was trying to drag her to the floor. Like Leda, she had undergone extensive doctor-mandated testing that night. Her torso was bandaged under her shirt, thanks to several cracked ribs, and both of her hands were wrapped to cover up the split knuckles she'd earned from repeatedly punching their kidnapper. The doctor had diagnosed her with a mild concussion, for which she'd ordered Rachel to take a week's rest and report back in two days for a follow-up visit.

Leda understood none of what the doctor said, but Rachel's friend—the tall, thin man with the goofy smile who'd saved them—had very kindly interpreted for her after introducing himself as Wu Daud len Wu. Even after four hours in the small hospital (which they'd entered by ducking behind a dumpster in an alley), he was still patiently translating every word.

The doctor's cell phone began to buzz and she excused herself for a moment. As she stepped into the hall, Wu said something to Rachel and then ducked out. As his footsteps faded away, Rachel walked stiffly to Leda's side and took a seat next to her on the hospital bed.

"How are you doing with all this?" she asked, her voice heavy and drawn.

"I'm alive," Leda said. "The rest of it I haven't thought about much."

"That's fair."

"Will I be able to go home soon?"

*

"I hope so."

Leda craned her neck to try to see into the hallway. "Where'd your friend run off to?"

"Wu? He's gone to check on Suarez."

Leda nodded. She had met Suarez—or, as he'd introduced himself, Suarez Viotto len Halla—only briefly before leaving the psychopath's house. Her first thought upon seeing him was that he was a soldier: he was fit, had sharp eyes, and walked with an air of command. Immediately upon arriving, he took charge of the scene and neither Rachel nor Wu questioned his right to do so. He used the unconscious kidnapper's own rope to tie him up and started making phone calls as the other three made their exit—Rachel shuffling slowly, Leda hopping on one leg and relying on Wu to hold her upright.

Something on the floor stirred, drawing Leda's attention. It was the old brown coat. As she looked on, it dragged itself to the far side of the room, where it settled down in a heap and became still once again.

Leda pointed her chin at it. "That's the daemon I saw before?"

"Yeah," Rachel said.

"Is it like a pet or something?"

"No," Rachel snorted. "It's defective. It was part of my work assignment for the week, but because the department is so busy, they told me to watch the thing until they free up some resources to deal with it."

"Part of your work assignment," Leda repeated. During their hours at the hospital, in between tests and doctor conversations, Rachel had explained the daemon monitoring system. As she silently absorbed the information, Leda reflected how dramatically her life had changed in one day that she could accept Rachel's words as truth rather than the ramblings of a lunatic. "Like arresting that man was part of your work?"

"Yeah. And finding you, although I didn't know it until that freak called you a gatekeeper. Even hearing that, I wouldn't have believed him if the daemon hadn't said that it saw something unusual in you."

Leda sifted through her jumbled memories of the kidnapping and recalled hearing the word *gatekeeper*, but only now, with the danger past, did she wonder what it meant. "What is a gatekeeper?" she asked. "What does it have to do with me?"

"A gatekeeper," Rachel said, "is like a placeholder for a daemon."

"Placeholder?"

"Yeah. See"—Rachel rubbed her bandaged ribs—"a long time ago, a daemon called Apep became defective in a dangerous way and my people, for whatever reason, were unable to repair it."

"So it went to the wastes." Leda remembered the winking black eyes in the orange bog with a shudder. "That place you mentioned before."

"Yes. But there's a problem: daemons move freely through dimensional barriers."

"And walls," Leda added, eyes darting to the old coat.

"The only way to keep Apep and others like it from drifting back into this world is to remove its ability to pass through borders. We have a technology that allows us to remove the part of a daemon that gives it interdimensional access, but we can't just take that piece and throw it away, because it might find its way back to the daemon. Historical records show that we tried a lot of different methods of keeping the daemons and their transdimensional abilities apart, but in the end the only effective way was to put the severed abilities in human beings."

"Put the pieces into people?" Leda asked, eyebrows raised. "How?"

"I don't know how it works," Rachel admitted. "Above my pay grade. But it's effective because a human body is incapable of moving through dimensions without a passage. Humans can carry the daemon's ability their whole lives without ever being able to use it, so that piece of the daemon stays safely separated from its former owner. It's a pretty neat little system."

Leda sat quietly a moment, digesting what she'd just learned. She knew it should be an overwhelming thing to hear, but after everything she had been through and everything she had learned tonight, this seemed small by comparison. However, it did beg one question.

"So," she asked with some slight hesitation, "I've got some daemon in me?"

"I wouldn't say 'in you,' exactly, but yes, more or less," Rachel said. "It doesn't affect your life in any material way, though. You're just carrying around a piece of the daemon Apep like most people carry around a birthmark or a scar."

A birthmark. A scar. A piece of a daemon. Leda's eyes drifted to the empty coat. A memory of the basement intruded into her thoughts, showing her an image of the coat with blood splatter down its front and long strips of human skin hanging from its collar. She winced. *There's a piece of that in me?*

"But who the hell gave this thing to me?" she snapped. "I didn't sign on for it!"

"One of your ancestors did."

"My ancestors?"

"An Egyptian aristocrat's daughter, according to our records." Rachel shifted her weight, grimaced, and gently held her sides. "Her father performed yearly rituals at a temple to banish Apep from the kingdom, so I guess she seemed like a good fit. She accepted the duty, and, when she had children, the piece of Apep duplicated and passed on to her daughters and granddaughters. Every girl born into that family who was a descendant of the first woman inherited a copy of it. In that way, the original ability divided and spread over the world, meaning that as long as there was one living female descendant of the first woman, it would stay safely separated from the daemon." She drew a ragged breath and held her ribs as she shifted position again. "Unfortunately, the direct female lines have dwindled over the millennia. Most of the lines either died out or had only male children. Then, just recently, the last recorded female descendants died. If they had been the last anchors holding pieces of the daemon in this world, the transdimensional ability would have returned to its source. Since that didn't happen, we knew there must be another female descendant somewhere. My job was to track her down."

"And that's me?"

"Looks that way."

"'Looks like way'? So you don't actually know," Leda said skeptically. A glimmer of hope that maybe she could go back to living a normal life flashed in her core. "I might not be this gatekeeper person."

"Well, actually . . ." Flinching from the pain of the movement, Rachel fished her cell phone out of her pocket, activated it, and showed Leda a screen full of foreign words.

"This," she explained, "is a message from a guy I know in our records department. He told me a few days ago that we had a record of one of the direct female lines going dead in

West Africa several hundred years ago, but there was one girl who was unaccounted for. He wrote me today to say he managed to dig up records of a slave auction in Virginia less than six months after that girl disappeared. An African girl was sold at that auction who was about the same age as the missing child. He followed up on the sale and found only one other mention of the girl, made almost twenty years later in a ledger kept on the plantation to which she was sold. It mentions her by the name 'Sarah' and lists her as having three children: two sons and a daughter. The daughter's name was"—she checked the screen of her phone again—"Ruthrose. Hmm. Unusual name."

A bolt of frost rippled through Leda as if a ghost had just whispered in her ear. "Oh my God," she said in a hushed whisper. "My grandmother told us about Ruthrose when we were little. She told us what her mother had told her, and her grandmother before that, and . . ." She licked her lips. She felt unsettled, like a still pool rippling from a tossed pebble. "She told us what Ruthrose told her daughters, what her mama had told her—that our family was important. She said . . . our *daughters* were important."

Overwhelming emotion broke open inside Leda's chest at the thought that her abduction was linked to an ancestral abduction that had taken place hundreds of years earlier. The immensity of it all overloaded her, and she slumped under its weight. "God," she said, "I don't know what to think. I just . . . don't."

Rachel watched Leda silently, allowing her the space to process the overwhelming knowledge she'd just been given.

Wu reappeared in the doorway and said something to Rachel in their incomprehensible language. Then he stepped aside to let Suarez and another man Leda did not recognize into the room.

The moment Rachel saw the second man's face, she sat up straight, her expression both tense and relieved. Suarez handed Rachel a faded blue container, no bigger than a shoebox, that was covered with stickers. As she accepted it, the other man— older and balding, with sunken brown eyes—spoke to her in their strange language. The man gestured toward Leda a few times while talking, but it was a while before he paused long enough for Rachel to translate what he was saying.

"The man who attacked us has been locked up," she finally told Leda. "There were trace amounts of human blood all over that basement and the closet was full of knives and . . . other things. They were all designed for the purpose of opening a passage through dimensions via ritual murder."

The two women locked eyes, a moment of horror frozen between them. They had come very close to joining those stains on the concrete.

"Who is he?" Leda whispered.

"He had eight or nine different IDs in his house, all of them fake, and the name on the deed of the house belongs to a man who hasn't been seen in years. There's no way to know for sure who he is unless he tells us."

"And he's not going to do that." Leda sighed.

"Probably not," Rachel confirmed. "It's not our top priority anyway. Some colleagues of mine are working to repair the damage he did to the dimensional barrier, but it'll take some time. Once that's dealt with, they'll figure out how best to alert Notan authorities about the girls who were murdered there. The Notan victims are for the police to deal with."

"And . . . him?" Leda asked.

"He stays with us," Rachel said firmly. "He claims he's working with Arcanans to illegally open a passage, so there's no way we're turning him over to Notan authorities. He'll face judgment for his crimes in our dimension."

"When?"

"As soon as possible."

"Will we have to testify at the trial?"

"There's no trial," said Rachel with a shake of her tired head. "He's not a citizen, so he's not entitled to one, but even if he was, there's no defense he could possibly use to mitigate what we've got against him." She leveled her gaze at Leda and drew her lips into a thin line. "There's no trial, just sentencing and, believe me, he will get the maximum." She closed her eyes and, gently nodding her head, exhaled slowly. "He's taken his last breath of free air."

An unwelcome flash of the kidnapper's face crossed Leda's mind; the sneer on his face stirred a nauseous panic in her. She shoved the image away and hugged her arms over her chest.

"Good," she muttered. "I hope he never sees daylight again."

The balding man addressed Rachel once again; Leda listened silently but intently, though she still couldn't translate a single word.

"MS. WILDE," MR. Vang said, "the Central Office still has some questions for you and your handling of this case."

"My 'handling' of it?" Rachel cocked an eyebrow. "What are you talking about?"

"This woman," he said, nodding at Miss Morley, "should never have been brought into this business. She's Notan.

Granted, she turned out to be a gatekeeper, but you could not have known that at the time you consulted her. Furthermore"—he pulled a phone from his pocket and checked its screen—"we had someone stop by your assigned residence, and there appears to be another Notan living there." He turned the phone toward her, showing an image of a young blond man with electric blue eyes. "This man."

"He's an oracle."

"Regardless, he doesn't belong in that house." He fixed her with a cold, accusatory stare. "Your interaction with these people is unacceptable."

Rachel met his gaze without flinching. She blinked slowly and tilted her head just slightly. "You sent me after a serial killer," she said, her voice pure steel. "You sent me after him unarmed, with no backup—and no way to call for help, since the offices were closed."

They continued to stare into each other's eyes as the seconds ticked by, neither yielding to the other's will. After what felt like minutes, Mr. Vang cleared his throat and glanced away, breaking the tension.

"All right then," he said casually. "Since the doctor wants you off your feet for a week, I'm assigning you to bring this woman and her family up to speed on gatekeeper history and protocol. I expect you to forward any information you gather on them to the records department."

He focused his attention on his phone, scrolling through something that was seemingly of great interest, while the three collectors exchanged knowing glances. Wu hid a smirk behind his hand, and Suarez nodded sharply at Rachel, who shrugged and exhaled in a puff.

"Fine," she said.

Mr. Vang nodded and sniffed, eyes still on his phone. "That just leaves the matter of this daemon," he said, pointing at the crumpled old coat. "The prisoner has a sizable bite wound on his hand that seems to have come from a daemon's mouth. As you know, a daemon cannot inflict physical injury unless it has at least partially crossed into this dimension. Was this daemon the culprit?"

"Yes."

"And this is the daemon we charged you with safekeeping?"

"It is."

"I see," he mumbled. "Well, that means our assessment of the daemon may have been incorrect. If its defect is serious enough that it can bite a human, then it will need to be sent away immediately."

"That's fast," Rachel said, surprised. "Doesn't it usually take weeks to make a wastes-related decision?"

"Normally, yes. However . . ." He took a deep breath and lifted his gaze to meet hers. "During the systems check, we are shorthanded and low on resources, and now, with this prisoner claiming that he's in league with a group of Arcanans, we can't afford to waste time on a lengthy decision-making process." A glint of concern shone in his eyes, startling Rachel. "If what the prisoner says is true and there really are Arcanans who are willing to commit murder to break down dimensional barriers, then we have bigger problems to deal with than one defective daemon. If the daemon is dangerous enough to physically attack a human, then it will have to be fast-tracked."

"Right," Rachel said. "But it's not defective."

Mr. Vang squinted at her; out of the corner of her eye, Rachel saw the peculiar expressions Wu and Suarez were casting in her direction.

"Oh?" Mr. Vang said.

"Well," she backtracked, "it *is* defective, but . . ."

Rachel glanced at the coat-covered daemon. The invisible thing was hunkered down within its cloth armor, seemingly oblivious to the fateful conversation taking place just a few feet away. It had not spoken in hours, and Rachel had not said a word to it about what had happened in the basement, and yet she felt that they had reached an understanding. It hadn't chosen to be defective, just like it hadn't chosen to be placed in her care, but it had chosen to come to her rescue when she needed it. She hadn't chosen this daemon as her assignment, and she hadn't chosen to have it follow her around like a semi-tangible shadow, but she could choose to return the favor it had done her. Besides, after all she'd been through, she didn't feel too guilty about lying to the Central Office right now.

"It's defective," she said, "but it's not dangerous. I told it to bite that man."

"Really?"

"Yes. It was following me around because of something I said—a slip of the tongue—and it ended up following me into that guy's basement. When things got scary, I told the daemon to bite him to buy us some time. I mean," she pressed, "you guys handed the daemon to me to monitor its defect, right? If it's obeying my orders, then the defect can't be all that bad."

Mr. Vang looked long and hard at the coat on the floor, as if waiting for it to speak on its own behalf. Suarez maintained a solid expression but shot Rachel an unspoken question with his eyes. Wu looked back and forth between the daemon and Rachel several times before shaking his head and shrugging. The daemon didn't move.

"Hmm," said the older man. "If what you say is true, then the daemon can remain under your supervision. Frankly, it will be less trouble for us if it does. We have our hands full with every kind of trouble at the moment."

"Is that why the office was closed?" Rachel asked.

"Yeah," Wu chimed in, "what's the deal? Since when do you guys not answer the phone?"

"I have no answers for you, just as I had no answers for Mr. Reuben, who called us incessantly on your behalf," Mr. Vang said. "We have an overload of defective daemons, our entire division is being subjected to procedural scrutiny, and then, without warning, our communications went down. Yesterday I would have called it an unfortunate coincidence, but now, with all we've heard from the prisoner, I wouldn't swear to it." He sighed and shook his head. Rachel noticed beads of sweat at his temples. "Sabotage is quite possible."

Wu and Suarez exchanged a confused, worried look, the expression of an emotion Rachel shared but was too tired to wear on her face.

"What's being done about it?" she asked.

"There are . . . procedures in play."

"There are procedures for this sort of thing?"

"Well . . . no," Mr. Vang admitted. He threw out his arms in a gesture of exasperation. "We're making it up as we go at this point. The Notans have procedures for this sort of . . . conspiracy . . . terrorist threat, so we're adopting their procedures as guidelines."

"Terrorist?" Miss Morley exclaimed. It was the first time she'd made a sound since this conversation began, probably because Mr. Vang had said "terrorist" in English. "What's that about?"

"We even have to borrow a Notan word for the concept," Mr. Vang said in Arcanan.

"That's gotta be a first," said Suarez.

"First or last is immaterial when the matter is at hand," Mr. Vang said with an air of finality. "Well, now that all of this is settled, I'll leave you in the doctor's care. Good night."

He nodded quickly to the three collectors, avoiding eye contact, and then speed-walked out of the room.

Suarez ran both hands through his hair and grumbled wearily under his breath. "Terrorism," he said. "Can't be."

"Terrorism?" Miss Morley poked Rachel's shoulder to get her attention. "What the hell's going on?"

"The prisoner said some things that suggest a terrorist group may be behind recent events," she replied.

"Ah, come on!" said Wu with a wave of his hand. "We're gonna take the word of a murderer?"

"I'm not," Rachel said. "I don't trust anything that comes out of that man's mouth."

"But you said he knew things about us," Suarez pointed out. "You said he knew things about the Arcana."

"That doesn't mean there's terrorism involved," she said.

"Then how do you explain it?"

"I don't. I'm not coming to *any* conclusions based on something that psycho said."

"Sounds sensible to me," Wu said.

"Still," Suarez said, "it's concerning."

Wu clapped him on the shoulder. "Don't look so serious," he teased. "We caught the guy, Wilde's safe, and the office is open again. It's all good!"

Suarez folded his arms over his chest and stared at the floor, his face a haze of deep thought.

Wu rolled his eyes, looked at Rachel, and shrugged. "I think we're done for the night, Wilde. We're just getting underfoot at this point. We should probably dash."

"Okay," she said. "Thanks, guys. For everything."

"No thanks necessary," Suarez said. Clearly still lost in contemplation, he lifted his head just long enough to offer up a brisk nod before turning to the door. "Miss Morley. Later, Wilde."

"Hey," Wu added over his shoulder as he followed Suarez to the exit, "Benny said we're meeting at his place for dinner next week."

"I'll be there," Rachel said.

"Can't wait to hear this story from your end. See you soon, Wilde."

"Later."

They left the room one after the other, and Rachel listened to their fading footsteps until they were too far away for her tired ears to follow.

"What was all that about?" Miss Morley asked. "Was that guy your boss?"

"Sort of." Rachel sighed. "He's from the Central Office."

"Sounded like he's pissed at you. Everything okay?"

"Yeah. He won't harp on my mistakes if I don't mention his. Anyway, this is for you."

She handed Miss Morley the blue box Suarez had given her. It was covered in handwritten labels.

Miss Morley peeled back a few stickers and removed the lid. The box was full of flash drives, CD-ROMS, and other data storage devices. Her eyebrows pinched together as she stared at the box's contents. "What is this?"

"It's yours," Rachel said. "It's everything we have from the Apep gatekeeper bloodline."

"So it's . . . records?"

"Some of it. It's more files like the ones I brought you before."

"The diaries?"

"Yeah. Apparently, your ancestors have been keeping records of their lives and their children's lives for almost as long as they've been carrying this gatekeeper mantle. Those diaries you read were written by your distant relatives." Rachel flipped over the lid of the box, where several scribble-covered stickers overlapped each other. "Not clear how some of it ended up in that psycho's house—I mean, all of this should have been kept in the records department—but from the look of it, it was shuttled around to a bunch of places." She scraped back the corner of a sticker. "Looks like it got sent to . . . Barvekaj, which is weird, because that's where dangerous things—weapons and problematic tech—are stored. Then it went to . . . the Research and Development Department, then to the military, and then to a village in the far west and then to . . . eh." She tossed the lid aside. "Forget it. It's back where it belongs. Your ancestors wrote these, and someone converted them to digital form. The box belongs with you."

"My ancestors?" Miss Morley repeated. Her voice was hushed, breathless. Her dark eyes shifted between doubt and hope. "You're sure? There's no mistake?"

"It's yours," Rachel said. "It belongs to you and your family."

Miss Morley pushed around the items in the box with two bandaged fingers. "There are so many," she murmured.

"That flash drive I brought to you was originally part of this collection. That one memory stick, as it turns out, has the last written records from your ancestors on the west coast of Africa. The last matriarch of that line sent her distant cousins a message about her missing granddaughter, and that message was digitized with the other records. That was probably why that psychopath wanted it—it was the only thing in the box that had any useful information about your branch of the family tree. It was his only hope of tracking you down. Well." She flinched. "Until I led him to you. Sorry about that."

"That's . . . I . . . ." Miss Morley's voice trailed away. After some long moments had passed, she covered her lips with her wrapped fingers. A tear dropped into the box, creating a tiny, discolored spot in the blue cardboard.

Startled, Rachel bent her head to better see Miss Morley's face. Her dark eyes were brimming over with tears. Rachel carefully placed one hand on her shoulder. "Are you okay?"

"Yeah," Miss Morley sobbed. "Oh my God, I'm fine. I . . . shit! I don't like to cry," she hissed. She swiped at her cheeks and clenched her trembling lips tight together. A strangled cry came from deep in her throat, and she let fall a shower of tears. "I don't know," she sobbed. "I don't know."

Rachel didn't fully understand why Miss Morley was so overwhelmed but, exhausted as she was, she could appreciate the need for a release. It had been a traumatic evening; they both had wounds—outside and in—that needed tending. Add to that the fact that she had just been reconnected to her gate-keeper heritage, and Rachel could guess that there was a lot going on in her mind.

"That's okay," she said. She squeezed Miss Morley's shoulder and smiled faintly, a smile lacking in comprehension but as full of compassion as she could make it. "I think it would be asking too much of you to ask that you get a grip on everything all at once."

Miss Morley nodded without lifting her head. Tears continued to roll down her face, half-hidden by a curtain of her hair. "I don't know where to begin." She put one shaking hand into the box and brushed her fingers over the data. "There's so much stolen history in here that I never dreamed I'd find. It's so much, and so precious. So many years, so many relatives . . ."

"And so many languages!" Rachel said with another smile. "You're a linguist! It's like you've been preparing all your life to get this box!"

In the midst of her tears and soft cries, Miss Morley laughed. "I have," she laugh-sobbed. She gripped the box in her trembling hands as if afraid it would fade away. Her cheeks were soaked with her tears, but in between sobs she smiled and glanced skyward. "Thank you, Jesus. Thank you for getting me ready for this." Her face softened, suddenly peaceful. "And," she said softly, "thank you for today."

17

CRAWLSPACE

It was late when Rachel finally shuffled through the passageway and up the walk to her house. As she stepped over the
nothingness threshold, leaving her long night behind, she was
greeted by the buttery glow of the porch light. Despite the
pain, she inhaled deeply. An earthy aroma, the comfortable
smell of this place, filled her senses. She tilted her head back
to see a spread of stars above. There were no familiar constel-
lations in this sky, but the tiny lights were soothing. The job
was done. She was done. She could rest.

Her body stiff and aching, she slowly climbed the porch
steps. It sucked that she had to let her injuries heal naturally. If
she had been injured back home, she would have been patched
up in a matter of hours, but since the interdimensional passages were currently sealed, the Arcanan doctors who had
treated her were cut off from modern technology and allowed
to use only things that would not be seen as unnaturally ad-
vanced if discovered by Notans. That was all well and good for
security, of course, but it left Rachel in a lot of pain.

Five more months, she thought. *Just five more months until I
go home.*

Pulling herself to the top step, she limped a few steps
across the porch and pushed open the door. Behind her, the

daemon hopped up the steps; the fabric wrapped around it dragged over the wood as it slouched its way inside. She waited for it to enter and then closed the door. Without hesitation, it shuffled away and out of sight, its old coat softly rustling.

The moment the door clicked shut, she heard Bach call out, "Hey!" from upstairs. He rushed down the steps and greeted her with a too-eager smile that drained her last drop of energy. "Glad you're back."

"Yeah?" she muttered, letting the coat draped around her shoulders fall to the floor. "Why?" She headed for the kitchen without waiting for a response.

"Some people came by while you were gone," he said, following behind her. "They seemed pretty pissed to see me."

"That's because you aren't supposed to be here," she reminded him.

"I know. They left pretty quick but . . . I didn't know what to say."

Rachel started to reach for a glass in the cabinet, but the movement sent a sharp pain through her side; she froze and hissed through her teeth.

Bach snatched the glass from over her shoulder and filled it with water.

"What did you tell them?" Rachel asked tightly, waiting for the pain to subside.

"The truth." He handed her the glass. "I even threw in a few sight-beyond factoids from their lives to prove it."

"Good," she murmured, very slowly lowering herself into a chair. She leaned back, wincing. "I don't think they'll come by again anytime soon."

Bach continued to hover about the room. Though he turned in every direction, his feet marching him from one corner to the next, his eyes kept darting back to her. Suddenly, he blinked, pulled back, and said in a surprised tone, "You don't look so great."

"Well, that's just as well," she said, "because I don't feel so great."

Bach took a seat across from her. "What happened?"

She recounted the events of the evening, beginning with her stakeout of Leda Morley's office and ending with their discharge from the hospital. Bach listened to every detail, never interrupting and never looking away. While Rachel talked, the daemon wandered aimlessly into their midst. It bumped against the edge of a cabinet, adjusted its course by an inch, and then parked itself under the table. The soft swish of its blood-splattered coat came to an abrupt stop as it ceased all movement and became as still as the table above it.

"How bad's your damage?" asked Bach once Rachel had reached the end.

"Cracked ribs, concussion, a few lesser injuries," she told him. "I'm gonna hurt for a while, but it could've been much worse."

"It's my fault, isn't it?" He groaned. "I sent you there in the first place."

"You didn't know. Besides, it all worked out. We caught the guy, and Miss Morley's been identified as the missing gatekeeper. I probably wouldn't have found either one of them without your help." Holding her breath, she fished a pill sachet out of her pocket. She flicked the two painkillers into her mouth, took a long drink, and then leaned the glass against her heart while she swallowed. "Just don't expect a thank-you, okay? You helped me finish my work for the week, but you also got my ass kicked. I figure that balances out."

"Fair."

A sharp whine broke the air; startled, Rachel looked toward the hallway. A dog—a puppy, really, maybe six months old—lingered just outside the kitchen entrance, poking its black-and-brown head around the corner. Rachel looked at Bach, her eyes narrowed, and the young man smiled sheepishly.

"He was under your house," he said.

"I know," she said, her voice sawing into him. "I chose not to bring it in here."

"I'm sorry," he said. "I was . . . I like dogs. Always wanted one when I was a kid, but my mom said no. Just look how cute he is." When Rachel continued to glare at him, never glancing at the dog, he slumped forward and mumbled in a grim tone, "Sorry. After you left, I heard him whining under the house, so I gave him the last bite of my burger. I just wanted some company before you threw me out."

"I wasn't planning on throwing you out."

His face shifted into a meld of relief and amazement. "Really? But those people who came here were very clear about the rules—"

"I'm not too thrilled with the Central Office and its rules just now," she growled. "If they'd done their research properly, I wouldn't have landed in the hospital. Screw 'em."

Bach heaved a sigh and collapsed back into his chair, his arms hanging limp from his sides. "Thank God. I didn't know what I was gonna do."

"You can stay until the Central Office makes another stink about it," said Rachel. "They'll avoid revisiting my situation for a while after they so completely fucked up this case. I think you've got a couple months' leeway."

Bach lowered his chin, pressed his palms together before

his face, and exclaimed, "Thank you, thank you, thank you."

"But just so we're clear," she added, "I'm not feeding you or that animal. The roof over your head doesn't cost me anything, but I can't start charging food for two people and a dog. If the Central Office sees that kind of increase in my expenses, it won't matter how badly they screwed up this last job, they will have my head. If you want to stay, you buy your own food."

"I can do that," he assured her. "Just give me a few days and I'll get it all sorted out."

The puppy whined again, bobbed his head up and down in the doorway, shuffled his oversized paws back and forth, and glanced from one human to the other.

"What about the dog?" Bach asked. "Can he stay?"

"I guess," Rachel mumbled. "Just clean up after it and don't let it lift its leg to anything in the house."

"Come here, boy," Bach called. "Come here."

The puppy yipped with joy and rushed to the man's side. He gave the daemon a nervous glance, but his new master's command seemingly overrode that concern. He ducked low and brought his head up, directly into Bach's palm. The young man rubbed the dog's absurdly huge upright ears and scratched the back of its neck, drawing blissful groans from the animal.

Rachel rolled her eyes.

"Good boy," Bach whispered. "That's a good dog. I think he's a collie-shepherd mix," he told Rachel. "Can't be sure, of course, but he's got a collie build and these ears look shepherd-ish to me."

"Looks pretty well fed," Rachel mused as her eyes swept over the puppy. "Wonder what it was eating all this time."

"Oh!" said Bach, eyes wide. "Didn't you know? The crawl-space under this house is littered with stuff."

Rachel stared at him a moment and then closed her eyes and shook her head. "What?"

"Yeah," he said. "There are tons of food wrappers and empty cartons. There's also a lamp, a chunk of pavement, something that looks like a rice cooker, a couple of doorknobs, a sink faucet, a street sign with some weird language on it, a barstool, a—"

"What?" she shouted, grimacing in pain the moment the word left her mouth.

The daemon shuddered in response to Rachel's yell. Its movement startled the puppy; he tucked his tail, whimpered, and licked Bach's hand.

Bach cringed a little under Rachel's accusatory glare but continued, "And that little tree out back is actually a big vine. It's rooted under the house. Looks like it must've sprouted from a seed down there."

"That's insane," she said. "I had to do an inspection of this place when I moved in. I checked the crawlspace and it was empty."

"Not anymore," said Bach with a shrug.

"But who could've put that crap down there?" she asked no one in particular. "Who would sneak into a pocket dimension just to dump their trash?"

Bach's eyes flickered, and she realized he was searching his sight-beyond data banks for an answer.

"No one," he finally said. "I'm sure of it. No one was here."

"So how did it get under the house? How did all that crap end up here without someone carrying it through the passage?"

Bach stared at her strangely, as if she had said something

in another language. Then he shrugged. "I don't know," he admitted. "I know no one was here, but that's all I've got."

"I . . . oh, forget it," Rachel said. "I'll figure it out later."

The puppy scooted under the table and gently nudged her leg. She looked down and he wagged his tail. The tail whapped the daemon, softly thudding against the coat with each sweep. After five or six whaps, the daemon shifted its weight, startling the dog. He moved to the other side of Rachel's chair to avoid the invisible creature.

Rachel sighed. "Come here, you," she commanded.

The dog scampered out from under the table and stared up at her. She looked him over with a curious eye. His body was long and bony, and his white legs were gangly from youthful growth. His wagging tail had stiff bristles like a hairbrush, and when it came to a stop, it curled up, resting on his rump in a perfect O.

"Hmm," said Rachel, surprised. "It's not a mix."

"He's not?"

"It's a Noki," she said. "It's a herding breed. The tail and ears are a dead giveaway."

"So it's Arcanan? How'd an Arcanan dog end up under this house?"

"I guess the same way all that other stuff got there." Rachel pinched the bridge of her nose. "However that happened. I don't know. I'm tired, I hurt, and I don't give a shit. I'll deal with it all later."

She started to rise, winced, and sank back down. Bach jumped to his feet and flew around the table to help. She managed to pull herself up by holding on to his arm. Once she was upright, without a word, she gently pushed off of his chest and made her way into the hall.

BACH STOOD, WATCHING her go. Then, with a sudden jolt, he ran into the hall. Just as she mounted the first stair, he blurted out, "Hey!"

She looked at him, her eyes carrying the weight of her terrible night.

"Thank you," he said. "I, uh . . . I never had any right to expect your kindness. So thank you for it. If there's ever anything I can do . . . please tell me."

She smiled wearily, a smile that was polite but unconvincing, and nodded a little. Bach didn't need his sight-beyond to see that there wasn't an ounce of strength left in her to devote to him and his thanks. What little energy she still had was earmarked for the journey to her bed. Slowly, she continued her way up the stairs, one hand on the railing and the other clutching her bandaged ribs.

Bach's eyes stayed fixed on her. The sight of her labored climb filled him with a desperate resolve he had never felt before but now fully embraced. She had believed him. When he told her no one had come through the passageway to dump trash, she had accepted his word as definitive. It was a strange but amazing sensation to be believed despite not being able to provide any proof. He owed her too much to repay, and yet he had to repay it. He had to.

The puppy lingered at Bach's heels, his adoring eyes never leaving him.

Bach reached down and rubbed the animal's head. "Good boy," he crooned. "I'll take care of you. Don't you worry."

Back in the kitchen, the daemon sat under the table, still and oblivious.

EPILOGUE

He sat in the locked, windowless room and stared at the wall. He took carefully measured breaths while keeping his back flat against the wall behind him, the chill of the bricks biting through his torn shirt. His hand was heavily bandaged, but still the blood from his wounds seeped through. Bitten by a daemon wearing a woman's coat. The indignity of it turned his stomach. The only thing that kept him from dwelling on it was the greater indignity of having been defeated and captured in his own home.

Those two little bitches he had tried to hold in his basement were clearly to blame for this travesty. The gatekeeper had obviously been bait, while the other one had been sent to spring the trap. If all had gone as planned, there would have been fresh blood all over his basement, his tools, and his skin by now. Instead, he was locked in a cell, and the blood on his clothes and ruined hand was almost entirely his own. Those damn whores.

The Arcanans he worked with should have warned him ahead of time that a collector was after him. So far, he'd been waiting for them to show up, stalling by dealing out only tid-bits of information to his captors, but so far there was no sign of rescue. He snorted. To hell with them. He had no compunction about telling the Arcanan authorities about his allies if this was the best they could do for him. When the guards returned to his cell, he would give them more than the barebones facts that he had previously supplied. He would throw them all to the dogs.

With a bang that made him jump, the cell door suddenly opened. Through the poorly lit doorway, the prisoner's eyes fell upon a familiar face—one that did not belong to the men who had questioned him earlier. He smirked and his blood warmed with satisfaction.

"Decided not to leave me here, huh?" he taunted. "Do I know too much about you to be left unsupervised?"

"If that was true," said the Arcanan, "you'd be dead by now."

The words registered less as a threat than as a blow to his ego. His grin faded into a snarl.

"Don't fuck with me," he said. "You need me."

"Yeah," said the Arcanan, his tone one of blatant disgust. "We do." He curled his lip. "We wouldn't have gone near a sack of shit like you unless we had no other recourse."

"Watch what you say," he snapped. "If you piss me off, who's going to do the bloodletting you're too squeamish to do?"

The Arcanan shook his head and scoffed. "If you think being a murderer makes you special, then you're even more delusional than I thought."

He glared, his anger fueled by the fires of resentment and damaged pride.

Before he could say a word, his rescuer stepped back from the door and waved at him impatiently. "Get up," he ordered. "I'm taking you out of here."

He glanced up and down the hall as he exited. There was

no one in sight, and the Arcanan seemed unconcerned that they might be caught. Newly confident, he followed the other man through a maze of doors and hallways. Several times, as they passed through one empty room after another, his guide paused and held up his hand for silence, seemingly waiting for an unseen passerby to move out of their path.

By the time they reached the right door, they had encountered no one and had set off no alarms. The Arcanan opened the door onto a deserted street, a flickering lamppost casting irregular shadows over the cracked sidewalk. He held out a wallet and car keys. "Take your shit and get outta here. Don't go back to that house. We have a new location prepared for you. The address is in your wallet. Settle in there and keep a low profile—very low. The Arcanans will be after you now, and if they find you this time, they won't send just one unprepared collector. We'll do what we can to thwart their investigation on this end, but we can't draw attention to ourselves, so you'll have to be on your guard."

He sneered. "They won't catch me again."

"See that they don't." The Arcanan pointed up the street, gestured for him to start walking, and turned to head back into the dark passage.

He shoved his belongings into his pocket. "You know," he said, drawing the retreating man's attention, "all my work to open the passageway is gone. All those girls . . ." He grinned, his teeth gleaming in the stuttering light. "I'll have to start over from scratch."

The Arcanan stared at him over his shoulder with his nose wrinkled, as if he reeked of filth. After a beat, he hissed a breath through clenched teeth, returned a reluctant nod, and said coldly, "Then you'd better get to work."

ACKNOWLEDGMENTS

I'm overwhelmingly grateful to my husband, Matt, who has provided me with more love and support than I ever could have asked for. If not for his support and encouragement, I never would have found the courage to publish.

I'm always thankful for the love and brain-bending questions of my son, Eric. He gives me a lot to think about, changes my perception of the world, and makes me want to grow.

I owe a big debt to Eileen McFalls and the Women Writers of the Triad critique group. Their analysis of my work—from glowing praise to brutal-but-honest criticism—has made me a better writer.

A special thanks to Mrs. Webb, my sixth grade English teacher. I first began writing when she told me I had talent. Good teachers change lives.

Thank you.

ABOUT THE AUTHOR

Credit: Ivan Saul Cutler

ALISON LEVY lives in Greensboro, North Carolina, with her husband, son, and variety of pets. When she's not writing or doing mom things, she crochets, gardens, walks her collies, and works on home improvement projects.

Printed in the United States
by Baker & Taylor Publisher Services